The Ancient Device

The Ancient Device

Simon O'Sullivan

tp

Published in this First Edition in 2024 by:
Triarchy Press
Axminster, England

info@triarchypress.net
www.triarchypress.net

A catalogue record for this book is available from the British Library.

Print ISBN: 978-1-917251-01-3
ePub ISBN: 978-1-917251-02-0

For John Cowton and Ola Ståhl, both of whom saw some of themselves in this book; and Jon K Shaw who generously worked on a draft of it.

Thanks also to Justin Barton, Neil Chapman and Tom O'Sullivan for comments on an earlier draft; to Plastique Fantastique (in particular David Burrows, Vanessa Page and Alex Marzeta) for inspiration (especially in relation to Chapter 23); and to Phil Smith and Andrew Carey for their encouragement and support with the book's publication.

Contents

Four actors have I brought
Who were ne'er on a stage before;
But they will do their best,
And they can do no more

Prelude

Ribbonhead fetches the hurdy-gurdy from the cart, sits down on a tree stump and begins to play. His head is bowed as he leans into the drawn-out notes. It's a song of loss and sadness, haunting, off key. The tune transports them all to other times and places, in their past but perhaps in their future too? Hare is looking straight ahead, but his gaze is unfocussed and blank. John looks at his hands and rubs his palms together as if there is something coating them. Something that needs removing. Occasionally he lets out a low grunt. Fox-Owl is the only one still standing. He is busying himself about the camp and the cart, pulling the tarpaulin taught once more, seeing to the pots and pans, but all of this as if in slow motion. As if the tune has thickened the air.

Eventually Ribbonhead plays a final long note which then slowly backgrounds itself as the other sounds of the landscape come to the fore. Birds calling, the rustling of the breeze in the treetops. Something in the bushes perhaps—there is a further rustling there—that had also been listening (it wouldn't be the first time Ribbonhead's playing had called something forth). Ribbonhead puts the heavy instrument gently to one side and sits forwards, elbows on knees, his thin hands clasped in front of him, fingers touching.

'I've played that song for all of us here, those I can see and those I can't.' His accent is strong, a west country twang and sing song in its cadence. 'It's all I have to offer at this time—that is, until something else makes itself known.'

Fox-Owl has paused whilst these words are spoken, but then begins his tasks again with more urgency and, as he checks straps and ties, he also speaks. 'It may well be that nothing will become apparent to us. We need to face that possibility. That this, simply, is our lot. That we must now make do.'

Ribbonhead turns his head towards Fox-Owl but remains silent. John lets out a slightly louder grunt, rubs his hands more vigorously together and frowns, then looks up from under hooded eyes. 'Make do? What does that mean? There's now't here to make do with.' John's voice is gruff but not angry—there's no edge—just a sense of resignation.

'Why not play us another verse?' says Fox-Owl, although he does not pause in his work. 'And Hare, are you up for a song?' Hare twitches and turns his head. He looks at Fox-Owl, then at John and finally Ribbonhead. He nods quickly, strokes the back of his neck, then clears his throat. Ribbonhead reaches down and lifts the hurdy-gurdy like it's a small child, settles it on his knee and begins to play once more. This time there is a new sound wrapping itself around the notes as Hare's high-pitched voice joins in. The lyrics are unclear—as if Hare is singing in another language or, at least, a different dialect—but occasionally some words and, with those, also some images can be made out. It's a song about being lost and found. About being taken up by something very old and led somewhere else. There are different characters—even animals perhaps—each, it seems, with their own intonations which Hare manages to conjure. It's as if a further scene has been superimposed on this one here, a whole procession of ghostly figures acting out some other story. John has raised his head now and, cocking an eyebrow, is staring at the embers of the fire in the in the middle of their camp. Fox-Owl too has stopped and is also watching as this other narrative unfolds.

And all the time Ribbonhead keeps the handle turning, grinding out image after image. It's as if all of these other worlds and figures are there inside his instrument and Hare's song is helping coax them out. The hurdy-gurdy is not the device they are after, but it is something. It offers a pre-view or sketch, written in feeling-tones and now further outlined with the words of Hare's song.

All at once the performance is over. Ribbonhead is bowed even further over and Hare's last words have been spoken into the air.

Fox-Owl nods. 'That's a fine song and well delivered at this time and place. If all else fails there is a path there for you two at least.'

John lets out another grunt. Looks up at each of the others in turn, then bows his own head once more. 'And what about this bundle of rags here. Can you see a way for me?'

Fox-Owl is attending to the ropes and straps once more. There is a long pause before he speaks. 'Your way John is not for me—or any of us here but you—to clearly see. It's certainly a more complicated path.'

'That's an understatement' says John as he looks once more at his hands. Again, there is no anger. The music has drained all of that much as a deep cut on the body can draw blood from a face.

Eventually Ribbonhead gets up and walks to the cart. He gently wraps the hurdy-gurdy in an old blanket and places it in the back. Hare gets up, strokes the back of his neck and then begins to gather up his own bits and pieces. John is the last to get up, and with a long sigh rolls his own sleeping stuff and follows them to the cart.

There is a faint smell of something rotten in the air as they move off. Sulphur perhaps? It's not from them. They don't have anything like that with them, God forbid. Perhaps it's a memory? Something left over from the song? It follows them as their old nag of a horse takes the strain and each of them push and pull so as to get things moving. A bird calls shrilly as they leave the clearing that has been their home for the night. The whole episode has indeed been as a cut. A moment of clarity summoned by the fiction that Ribbonhead and Hare had together spun.

Part I

On the Road

Chapter 1: Parts and Props

It's early evening and four individuals have turned up. Copies of the scripts have been passed around and, as those attending flick through the pages, a figure who looks to be the director—or, at least, he is the least uncomfortable looking there—welcomes them all and makes a short speech.

'Welcome, welcome. So very pleased you have chosen to come along to be part of what I'm sure is going to be a transformative experience.' The other three look on in silence. There are a couple of raised eyebrows. The speech continues. 'As you can see there are only four main parts—well, really, only four parts in all—but two of the characters, Fox-Owl and Ribbonhead, can be played by several different actors. There are also scenes in which other figures step up to play their part, although, if we don't have the numbers', he looks around the room as if expecting to see more arrivals, 'then these are also parts that can be played by our main four.'

He pauses, looking pointedly at each of the other three in turn.

'At any rate there should be enough parts for everyone here.' Another pause. 'And then, of course, there are roles that need to be allocated especially for those who prefer', he coughs a couple of times, 'to be more behind the scenes, so to speak. Perhaps we might double up some of these too.'

One of the other three speaks up. A tall lanky figure, someone who has certainly seen better days. His hands gesture in the air as he speaks, slightly mumbling but then with some words clearly and precisely articulated. 'If no-one else feels like taking the part, then this fella Ribbonhead is something I'd be up for trying on.' He flicks through the script. 'Their speaking part is somewhat thin, but that suits me. And, I'm thinking, perhaps there's some scope for adlibbing here and there?'

There is a quietness and stillness. Things have begun to begin. The director nods vigorously and with a pencil he takes from behind one of his ears makes a note on the bundle of papers he holds.

A large, bearded man speaks next. He is rough looking, a bit battered and bruised. Feint blue tattoos on knuckles and wrists that are peeping out of shirt sleeves. 'I'll have a go at this King John character.' He frowns as he says this. 'I've always fancied myself as such.' He snorts. 'It seems a tragic part, but maybe I can bring something else to it, so it is less as such?' He looks at the director. 'At any rate I've got a feel for what a king might be like, precisely because I ain't one. In fact, I'm about as far as you can get from any kind of throne.'

'OK, good, good', says the director nodding and making another note. 'Now what about this character Hare?' The director is asking this but it's clear there is only one there for whom this part is intended (in fact, there's only one person left). A smallish and somewhat frail looking figure. As with all of them there is something a little misplaced about them as if they have turned up at the wrong place and at the wrong time.

'What about you? the director asks, nodding at this third individual. 'I'd say you have something of the hare about you—although, let's be clear, this is a play and we'll be acting, so how you seem and what part you play do not need to match. Indeed, in many ways, having a disjunction between these two allows all sorts of other things to come in to play.' He pauses and tilts his head slightly. 'Which amounts to saying there needs to be less of an identification with your parts.' As he says this last line the director glances around at the other two there.

Soon-to-be-Hare lets out a sigh and nods.

'Yes, I did recognise myself in some of what is written for this part, but then I recognise parts of myself in the other characters too.' He sighs again as he leafs through the pages of the script. 'But if this is all that's left then I'll give it a go. I'm certainly interested in the idea of scurrying around on all fours occasionally.'

'OK, good, good. That's nearly all decided then. There's just this character Fox-Owl who to be honest, is less a character and more a plot device in the play. For now, I'll take this on.' He nods a couple of times. 'Certainly, I am familiar with the directing role.' He smiles and moves his head from side to side. 'And it suits me to be wearing a mask which is what this role also requires. But let's see how we progress. Certainly, others can step up and into this part. I've no special claim to it.' Again, he smiles. 'Indeed, we can always switch things further around as we proceed.'

The director—or lets now call him by his other name—Fox-Owl, drags a big painted wooden box into the middle of them all. On each of the sides there are depictions of what might be landscapes with figures, although all of that is somewhat faded or painted in too dark colours to be properly make out.

'Now that the parts have been decided let's see to the props, such as they are.' The director lifts the heavy lid and one by one takes out the few props. First, it's a mess of ribbons tied to some kind of hat that is silently handed over to their new owner. Second a wooden crown, painted gold is handed to John who takes it with an appreciative grunt and a nod. Next a large animal type mask. Perhaps there is something of the fox and the owl about it, but cruder or certainly more abstract. It's made out of cardboard and tape. After that, the director takes out a smooth silver globe, about the size that will fit comfortably in the hand. Alongside that there is a wooden pole or staff and an empty green bottle. Finally, an old leather map case that has seen better days. All of these last few objects are laid out on the floor in front of them for inspection.

'What about me?' says Hare, 'is there no prop to help me get into my part?'

'Your part, as perhaps I should have mentioned earlier, is a little more complex and, you might say, all these props here.' Fox-Owl gestures to the array of objects on the wooden floor. 'And all of us characters in the parts that we will play—are your props. Certainly, there is a sense in which the action which we will soon rehearse is taking part in a place that is—how to say—located in your head. Simply put, all of us are to be thought of as figures conjured by you so as to work things out.' He gestures with his hands in a circular manner as he says this. 'Which is to say we are your own set-up.' There is a further pause before he adds seemingly as an afterthought, 'At least, that is one interpretation of our play.' A further pause. 'Another take is that each of us is a kind of set-up for the others to work things through.'

Chapter 2: Rehearsals

Fox-Owl has secured the use of the village hall for their rehearsals. It's a large building that might once have been a chapel of some kind. There's a dusty stained-glass window at the back, then in the main hall, there's tiered seating surrounding a stage of sorts. It's gloomy but not unwelcoming. Like other theatre spaces that are also village halls it has something slightly otherworldly about it as if it were from some other kind of fiction altogether. It is both an everyday thing—what village hasn't a hall like this?—and unusual. What are these village halls *for*?

'Well, here we are', says Fox-Owl, stating the obvious, but welcoming them anyway. 'This will be our home for the next while, except when the weather is clement, and then we might try rehearsing outside. At any rate, this is the space where we shall begin to work things out a little more.'

'It's a bit gloomy, are there not some lights?' says John who is holding the golden crown in one hand.

Fox-Owl replies. 'The gloom suits our themes. Too much light, at least early on, and the play risks taking on too much of a comic turn. We need the dark and the dusk so as to conjure the right mood.'

Hare pipes up. 'I suppose the twilight might also be dawn breaking?'

Fox-Owl nods. 'Yes, yes, you're right of course. The low light suggests not only the ending of the day but the beginning of another. Endings and beginnings. I think this is not necessarily a bad sum-up of this stage of things. At any rate, let's start and see how things go.'

Ribbonhead speaks from beneath the mess of ribbons falling over his head and shoulders: 'Have you the scripts? I don't see any papers in your hands...'

'There is no script for today. Instead, I have another idea to set things in motion and see what we are about. My suggestion for today is that we act out some material from our own lives. Perhaps even—if you can stomach it—something difficult and that you would rather not put on display if you take my meaning.'

John shrinks back. 'Hmmm. I'm not sure about this. I came along to play a part, not to be myself.'

'Well, in order to be able to take on another fiction, we first need to see more clearly the fiction that we are—or at least the edges of that anyway. There's no way around this. Otherwise, if we move too quickly then that other part will not only be less convincing to all, but, in fact, the real point—of acting something seriously out—will not take place. You need to trust me on this and follow my method.'

Hare is next to speak. 'I'm ready and willing but need more direction and some props. At any rate, I can't just drop into another state. I need a prompt.'

Fox Owl says. 'Of course, of course. And that is why we are here together, so as to operate as prompt—and, yes, possibly prop—for each other. Hare, how about you go first? Turn to one of us others here and make an observation. Now, what I mean by that is not just a description but your sense of what else is going on.'

There is a pause. It's not clear if Hare understands or, indeed, is willing or capable of taking these kinds of direction. But then he turns to the individual who is now Ribbonhead. 'Well, this figure here seems a little lost to me and, well, under nourished somehow. I hope I've not caused offence in saying this. It's as if he's not looking after himself or, perhaps, is wilfully bent on some dissolution.'

Fox-Owl speaks again. 'Good. Now then Ribbonhead—for that is what you are—act this out a little or, at least, allow it to provoke whatever comes. Remember, the method is to put the body in a certain position—to adopt the posture as it were—and then see what follows.'

Ribbonhead looks uncomfortable and even more stooped, but then he turns away from the rest of them and walks to the wall and stands facing it.

'Hare is right. I'm lost alright. It's what brought me here. It's this or back to the drink and all that entails. When I stand here and let what's been said in, it's almost unbearable.'

'Right, a good start' says Fox-Owl nodding quickly before turning to the figure who is to play the king. 'Now King John, what about this Hare here?'

John turns to Hare and speaks up. 'Well, they seem to me as if they are a hunted thing. There's a nervousness about them which, I'd say, goes deep. I imagine them a sick and wounded animal. No offence Hare, but you look, well, ill.'

Hare has visibly shrunk at these words and, indeed, has dropped to the ground and onto all fours and then curled in a ball. There's some noise—it is humming?—coming from him, but no words.

Fox-Owl speaks. 'Come on Hare tells us where you are.'

More humming, then some words, faint, a whisper almost, as if from very far away. 'I'm on that c-c-cold hill side, left all alone once more. There's nothing for me here. I'm waiting for an ending.'

There is a long pause. There they are, all of them figures as on a stage. And then Fox-Owl speaks. 'Right, now then, John, I have an observation to make. You seem to me as if you have indeed lost your crown or, at least, something precious. You walk around as if looking for something—though are also careful to hide this fact. Have I got that correct?'

John has been staring at Fox-Owl as he says these words. He then looks at Hare curled up on the ground and Ribbonhead with his face and body turned towards the wall. John looks at his hands, rubs them together, then speaks.

'Well, you've got me bang to rights there. I'd hoped to avoid all that by coming here, but now I see that there is no side stepping this business. These hands have let go of something alright. I'd cut them off if I had the courage.'

Fox-Owl speaks again. 'Good. Good. We now have a set-up of sorts to get us going. I know it's difficult but there's no other way. It's called acting but in fact, really, the opposite is the case. It's more real when framed in this way and put on display for all to see.'

John speaks up. 'And what about you Fox-Owl, behind that mask? What is it that you are about and can bring out of the shadows and on to the stage?'

'A good question John. For my lot I do not know exactly who I am or what I am about. Although my instructions to you were to feel as much as possible, for me it's more a case of witnessing and then taking on another's business.'

John frowns. 'Following your own instruction this sounds like avoidance to me.'

'You're right of course and perhaps that defines how and who I am to play. A flittering between this and that. An always being on the look out for other options. And behind all that, underneath this mask—or any other for that matter—well, it feels like there is nothing. Simply an emptiness where, perhaps a self might be expected to be.'

*

Fox-Owl had suggested the previous week that they do the next rehearsal outside if the weather would accommodate. It's a fine evening and as they arrive at the flat bit of grassland by the coast—which they had decided seems like an ideal place for this kind of thing—a golden sun is moving down towards the hills on the horizon. As they take up their positions there is a soft golden glow lighting up the few clouds in an otherwise blue and pink sky. Looking towards the horizon—which they are all doing now—the sun is beginning to settle on top of the hills, or rather, not settle exactly, but is rolling along them as if a wheel of flames. And now across the bay, the golden ladder appears on the rippling water, ready to be climbed by those who are willing and able. It's no wonder other times and other places had personified this sun. Certainly, it's as if it has decided to descend down and watch whatever it is that is going to transpire on the surface of this planet in this time and at this place.

Fox-Owl has given out the scripts and is just about to start with the directions, but then pauses and cocks his head. There is a soft drone coming from their left and off towards the sea.

'Can you all hear that or is it just my old, feathered ears that are manufacturing the drone?'

'I can hear it alright', says Ribbonhead. 'Sounds like it's more than one of whatever it is.'

Ribbonhead is right. As they listen the soft drone breaks down into a number of voices. A chant of sorts coming over the dunes and marshes to reach them there. It's a strange song, half tones and repetitions, building in speed then, as it reaches a crescendo, slowing down almost to a dirge. They can see the figures walking along the coast now towards them, perhaps twenty or so, all dressed in pale washed out clothes, men and women of different ages, some with instruments the sounds of which, now they can be seen, can also be made out within the different layers of the song. They're walking in single file along the beach, treading carefully in their bare feet. It's as if they are singing to the sea, but also to the sun which is just now beginning to dip slightly below the horizon.

Is it the tones or the voices or something else that begins to open up our four players assembled there? It summons feelings as if from nowhere or, perhaps, from out at sea or the hills above. Feelings that threaten to sweep them all up and away, but not with a violence exactly, more a kind of softness that can break open even the hardest heart.

John, who has his crown on now, speaks. 'It seems we are not the only ones out tonight for a performance.' His voice is softer than useful and although he intends to say these words as if it's a jokey comment his voice is hushed.

'Yes', says Hare—who is crouching down in the long grass—'we are blessed to have such a visitation before our first rehearsal. It's a good sign this!'

'Well', says Fox-Owl, 'it certainly seems a spell is being cast around and about this evening and that we have all become caught up in its workings. It has always occurred to me that magic and performance have a very special relationship.' He turns to look at the setting sun. 'And that any performance is always the outward manifestation of an inner transformation that it accompanies.'

'Surely that's enough philosophy for one night', says John as he watches the figures pass close—perhaps a couple of hundred yards away—and then walk on. Each of them is wearing the same baggy clothes, though there is not one style, more as if the apparel has been picked up second-hand, perhaps from charity shops and the like. And their hair, not long but not short either, cut into a certain

16

rough shape, with care but also it seems with a lack of interest in whatever the current fashions might be. They are certainly a random collection. But they also appear a cohesive group, clearly joined together with one or more invisible threads. None of them look at our players, focussed as they are on their journey—whatever that might be.

Perhaps this group of figures is from another fiction? They follow their own trajectory, inhabit their own narratives which, here, are situated in the same place, at least for a time. Is there an intersection between the two groups? Do they register Fox-Owl, Ribbonhead, King John and Hare? What are they for them? Ghosts from another time? Or are they simply further features of this landscape they move in and through, figures conjured by them and their song. Signposts that they are indeed, on the right track.

'Yes, enough philosophy' says Fox-Owl. 'It is time now to speak our parts and see what this landscape here might offer to our play (if indeed it is a play that we are to perform). One thing that strikes me as perhaps a useful conceit is to imagine that this here is the round.' He gestures with both arms to include the whole of the bay and the hills beyond. 'And that we are ourselves here to make a little scene that is nested within this larger landscape—which is to say our play is to be a device of sorts within this larger device, even if there are only the birds and beasts here to witness what transpires.'

There is some frowning and at least one shaking of the head. They've heard Fox-Owl waxing lyrical like this before and are becoming used to his claims for what they perform, claims that it seems—to the rest of them—are out of kilter with the little they have to offer.

Chapter 3: A Precursor

It's night-time. Hare, John and Ribbonhead are sat around their small fire. There is a stillness and a quietness to this small scene.

And then, from behind one of the stones, a fourth figure appears.

They are tall and stooped, stumbling slightly as they walk, though every now and then they straighten up to reveal a height of something like nine feet. A thin neck, even a pole perhaps, with a head on top or some such. And then it's clear that it's Fox-Owl's mask up there, but, here, in this twilight, it's as if the mask is larger and darker somehow. There it is looking out, and there, below, a body wrapped in different layers of cloth, a long skirt down to the knees and two or three aprons, each of different drab colours. This thing which has now appeared has no arms or, looking again, perhaps the arms are wrapped tight to the body by the cloth. It takes some steps, swaying gently as if drunk or moving to the beat of some drum that only it can hear. Occasionally it tips its head forwards as if nodding or bowing to the others.

The others have stood up now and turned their heads to look at this thing. But there are no nods of welcome or even acknowledgement, more simply a staring at what has arrived and a watching to see what it might do. It moves in and out between the stones, not a dance exactly—it's too erratic and clumsy for that— but there is certainly some intention at work. And then it's moving towards the others, going to each in turn and making the odd nod again as if attempting to point something out to each of them in turn.

And then John, Hare and Ribbonhead begin to move in unison. They are surrounding this thing, arms outstretched. It's no longer quiet, there's whistles and shouts from them as if they are attempting to grab its attention or coax it somehow. And this thing turns and turns, trying to respond to the noises, although, it seems, there are too many of them for it to attend to them all.

The whole set-up is becoming more animated now. Hare is leaping from one spot to another calling out in a voice that is almost a squeak. Then John is also stepping from foot to foot, arms bent and moving up and down, pointing with fingers at this strange thing that is, now, beginning to move more fluidly and fluently. And Ribbonhead? He seems, in part, to be mimicking this thing's dance, swaying and nodding as he himself moves from foot to foot like some kind of instrument that has been wound up and set to go. The whole scene is as if a musical box has been started up. As if this stone circle is the platform. As if these figures are moving in synch to some other deeper mechanism. Jerky and awkward at times, and then suddenly fluent again—running along some secret track, round and round.

The moon is up now and shining a pale white light on this animated scene. It feels as if this whole performance is being played out for some audience, but there is no one here except the participants and even then, it's not clear how present they are. At any rate it continues—John with his dance, Hare clicking and leaping and Ribbonhead swaying and stepping from foot to foot—whilst this thing, master of them all or, perhaps, simply a prop that they have summoned—continues its nodding and swaying, every now and again turning full circle as if indeed it is on some magnet that reaches down deep below.

And then it's over.

As if, quite suddenly, the music had stopped.

The creaturely thing has stepped out of the round, back behind the stones and out of the spotlight of that moon. And once this component has gone the others too are as if switched off. Ribbonhead standing still, head slightly bowed. Hare crouched down, panting heavily, his breath visible in the night air. John collapsing on to his knees, also breathing heavily as his chest rises and falls.

*

It's even later now and they have built up their small fire and set up mats and blankets to sleep. Hare is busy with the pots making a stew that smells good in the cold night air. John and Ribbonhead are smoking rolls ups, sharing tobacco and papers. It's as if a spell has been cast or, perhaps, has been lifted? And here they are, just them, without all that other baggage that weighs them down so heavily. There's a slight rustle at the edge of the circle of firelight, and Fox-Owl is back. He seems smaller somehow in that light. But also, more contained and quieter, as if whatever happened earlier has also cleared something out. He comes and sits with the rest of them by the fire.

Chapter 4: The Players

Standing at the edge of a meadow and trembling ever so slightly, Hare swivels his head from side to side and nervously surveys the scene. Around his neck hangs a crude double of himself—a small carved wooden hare made from a clothes peg, sequins and beads for eyes, one larger than the other. Something in Hare's body is not quite right. Something inside of him is reacting to something outside. Is it the long grass or the end-of-summer light? Or perhaps it's some of the berries or mushrooms he has foraged from the hedgerow? His intuition is that the ratios of this and that are all wrong and have been for a while. But, nevertheless, here he is, still alive. Still on the lookout.

Later that evening, as with many others, he finds a shallow hollow at the edge of another field. A good place for the night. Safe he thinks. It's usually somewhere like this, or just under a hedge perhaps, so long as it's quiet and well out of sight.

Hare keeps going to avoid something that follows him close, but also, he sometimes thinks with a frown, might already be up ahead. Hare knows that this thing will eventually catch him. He can sometimes feel its pre-presence like a soft touch or breath on his face. Early in the morning, as he opens his sticky eyes, he has at times had a sense that this other thing has already been there, even that it has been lying silently besides him all through the night. It's this feeling of being haunted that motivates him to arrange his things as each day begins, laying everything out before him, so that he might once again work out his priorities.

Now that he is on his own again all this preparation is fluid and fluent. It's other people that make things difficult. It's when he has to say things out loud and in a voice that he sometimes does not recognise as his own that he can lose his way. Hence the stuttering and stammering that invariably occurs.

After a small fire has been lit, water boiled and all the other various rituals performed—and if he has had a good night and can get the required distance—he begins the process of closely examining his desires and fears, alert to what, he thinks, might be his alone and then what is, rather, simply the result of the conditions he was born into. Sometimes he wonders if there is a difference between these two. What is there about him that is, in fact, his alone? And then, what might there be—*in there*—that could be utilised to go beyond whatever it is that he is? Such an enquiry—painstaking, often excruciating—takes time. He is himself tired of it. But without this regular and careful analysis, Hare's compass cannot be set and he cannot know which way to move on.

And then when all this work has been done, he reaches for the pole that has been cut for this purpose and makes the markings in the ground, diagramming out an impression of his past and present and then also a possible future trajectory.

So much for the usual routine.

In fact, Hare thinks he can smell something different on the morning breeze today. Something apart from the dampness and the coming of Autumn. Yes, he is sure. Someone, somewhere, has made another sign, and, with that, a signal has been sent. A glimmer of hope brightens Hare's one good eye. It's all been worth it he thinks as he packs away his few things. A decision is made—although Hare is never quite sure whether these decisions come after he begins to move—and off he limps, over forest and field, lightened, for the moment anyway, by a renewed sense of purpose.

*

Hare is the first to arrive on the scene. Perhaps he is a line for us to follow? Perhaps even an escape route of sorts? He has his own issues, that's for sure, but at least he has made a decision (or, again, a decision has been made) to dance to his own tune (for him, there wasn't much of a choice). Is he heading somewhere in particular? Towards an encounter with some other thing? Certainly, he fears, it cannot but end badly. But then when does it not? And on the way, surely, a little meaning might be found. Let's hope so anyway.

*

Propping himself up against the rubble, Ribbonhead takes another swig from the bottle. This old quarry has been his room for the night and, no doubt, will be again for the night to come. He is drunk—or, at least, out of it—listening to the bird song and the gentle buzz of bees on this bright and early late summer morning. Over his face fall faded ribbons of different colours—Blues, Golds, Reds and Greens—some down to his neck, others to his waist. He nods as if falling asleep or, perhaps, in acknowledgement of some private joke.

Why does he drink? He tells himself it's so that he can connect with where he is—be present right here and now—and, also, crucially, so that he can *see* (which at least whilst he is drinking is sometimes the case), but the whole truth is darker than this. He drinks to disconnect from some distant pain, a reservoir of sadness that he has only in his dreams seen the surface of (and with just that glimpse had an overwhelming sense of its depth). He also drinks because of the boredom (which he knows is more or less his alone). Because things have changed around him just as he himself has changed. He drinks because with all of this he is increasingly invisible.

It wasn't always like this. Once he stood more proud, striding across field and dale and from village to town. He would often be welcomed, made to feel at home, especially when a festival or some other celebration was to take place (and over which he might well be asked to preside). On these days he would laugh and tell them all stories of where he'd been. Advertise his various wares. And then he would also join in with any dance, his ribbons a blur of colour in many a village hall. Connection was easy back then, with other people but also with the landscape he moved in and through.

Where did he come from? Is he the last of them or will there be others? Perhaps some of these questions will be answered as things progress. But what can be said at this point—what is already apparent—is that this particular Ribbonhead is a left-over. He is a

23

residue from some other time. It's this that gives him his air of sadness, but also his sight. He has this rare (and somewhat unpredictable) ability to follow those lines that in these times have become increasingly obscured. In fact, if he can wait this time out, he will, he hopes, once again be in demand as someone that can reorientate the lost. In this time however, and at best, he might be paid to find a lost trinket or with less success cure a spell of gout.

After some more nodding he reaches into his jacket pocket and takes out a bundle of small wooden sticks and stares at them there in his hand. All of a sudden he throws them to the ground and looks for some moments at the jumbled pile made there. It's yet another attempt to see where he might be going with all this. How things might turn out. Alas, his sight is no longer strong enough to see his own fate, let alone that of any others.

But wait a minute.

He looks more closely at the pile.

There is something there. Something that the sticks have shaped. However, it needs encouragement. Ribbonhead takes another deep slug from the bottle and this time—he is surprised himself—begins to see. In amongst the jumble there is a pattern. A crude cone of sorts, its apex bisecting a flat plane and inside that shape a suggestion of other images that come thick and fast. All at once he is more present. Alert. He mutters to himself as if commenting on some internal process. '*Five miles away...I see it now...over hill and under wood...edge of field...a performance is taking place...a sign made...something else is stirring there...*'

And then, closing his eyes, he makes the stationary journey once more to this other place.

In no time at all he has arrived and watches from above as a figure that moves like a wounded hare makes their own marks in the earth before looking up as if they have seen something too.

And then, all of a sudden, Ribbonhead has returned and the seeing has, it seems, been done. After some more moments have passed he lets out a deep sigh, stretches out his long aching legs and gets to his feet. What a sight this is, a tall, stooped figure, a tangled mess of ribbons, stumbling around a disused quarry with an ungainly gait.

This Ribbonhead figure seems to be a marker of sorts. An indication of some other story, from some other time and place. He is also himself a performance, at least of some kind. An enactment of something different within this world that shows up its edges. His power—if he has any left—is that of the 'as if'. And he ceases to function when this set-up is seen through (and, perhaps the issue here, is that he is himself beginning to lose faith in his own fiction). He seems to be on the lookout for something. Watching out for his people perhaps? Or, at least, for those like himself that are a little washed up on the beach but not quite out for the count. Those who for one reason or another have been left behind. And it is just such a sign from just such a people that he fancies has at last been sent his way.

*

That same morning in a sparsely furnished room in a small house in a nearby town, Fox-Owl—although he is not quite that yet—fashions a mask from card, feathers, string and other bits and pieces he finds. At last, he thinks, he will assume a new name and this time it will be one of his own choosing. Why a fox and an owl? In fact, they had chosen him. Together they had visited one dark night and offered themselves up as materials for the making up of a new kind of thing come from an I-know-not-where to tell him of an I-know-not-what. These two animals are the needle and thread that will, he thinks, sew this new fiction together.

The mask he is making suggests that what follows is to be a performance, but then whatever else was this bundle that is sitting here punching holes in card and sticking tape fast? There was, it seems to him, always a series of masks, some of which functioned more or less adequately, others that had led to clichés and dead ends. It is only by shuttling through a particular set of options he has found—often through painful experimentation—that a little flexibility can be introduced into the situation. A little space opened up as it were around a self.

He needs to be prompted to make these different masks. Or, at least, he needs to be part of a scene that suggests this pursuit is a worthwhile thing to do (even if it's just him that's in it, which has often been the case). Context, he has found, is more or less everything. Sometimes the masks he makes have too much in them of what he already is. Although exaggerated, distorted perhaps, he recognises the face that looks back from the mirror. At other times the mask comes from too far off. It's just too strange. When it works, however, then there is a moment of surprise. A retrospective recognition that is also a non-recognition. 'Ah, so *that's* what I am and what I am *not!*' And, with that, it is as if a line has been drawn but also cast into the deep. Something else is finally in play. Something that was already there but obscured has revealed itself and stepped up to the plate.

Not to find a self then, but to make one. To try out masks and scripts and pick up props. To become a cause of yourself rather than be caused by some external agent, that is, indeed, his motivation (although he might not put it all quite like that). And, as such, to distrust anything that has the weight of reality. Anything that feels like this, finally, is the bottom. Instead, to understand any given self as simply a kind of backdrop against which other things play out. And, at all times to rail against interiority, or, rather, to see this interiority as simply one more fiction (and one that was certainly not of his own making).

To really become something different requires a certain kind of technique in which intention is used but also side stepped. There is no point, Fox-Owl has often reflected, in producing something that is recognisable to something already in place. Strange manoeuvres are required to make this other thing that will then speak back to you. Tell you what it is. But this first means some analysis is required. A laying bare of the constituents and components. A checking of all the cupboards and drawers. Seeing what's in there and then laying it all out for all to see. What might be repurposed and retooled? And what, when it comes to it, is just too far gone. Too, well, redundant?

The mask is done and now it's on his head. Fox-Owl (which is what he is now) lets out a short sharp bark. Up he jumps from the table and then he's scurrying down the stairs. Out of the door he goes then through the gate. Down the lane, leaping over a fence and off into the fields and open country beyond. Now, with this mask on, it is as if he is a quarry in a hunt.

Or, *perhaps*, he is to lead the hunt for some other thing?

*

Fox-Owl lives in the realm of images and language. It's where he moves (and what moves through him). But he is also an attempt to do a little scrambling—to make a little space—so that something else might come through. Something that might also surprise him at least. And perhaps, he thinks, this other thing might then also call those others close once more so that all of them together can try once more to find the way out from all of this.

*

Easing himself back in a battered old armchair, wood burner going, mug of hot tea in hand, King John looks out of the open doors of his truck that is parked up on a grassy verge. The view is of a pink and blue sky and a field of nodding corn. John coughs, stretches out his stiff legs, puts down his drink and rolls a cigarette. The skin of his hands is hardened and lined but his fingers are as dextrous as ever in performing this simple ritual. Blackbirds are awake now and calling to one another in the crisp dawn. There is a distant hum of traffic from somewhere not close but not that far away. John is content to be here, at this place, at this time, watching as the sun begins its morning climb.

He had decided—or something had—on a life on the road further back than he cares to remember. Certainly, whilst others were making their future plans and investing in this and that he had hitched his own destiny to the bus he bought with some savings and what was his small inheritance (he no longer remembers from whom). From shortly after that, through a gradual shift in position and perspective, he had become part of a community (at least of sorts). A rag tag band following a rough calendar of festivals and other less cohesive gatherings around and about.

John has dealt drugs—and occasionally still does—although he is a little more careful now not to be the only one there with a pocket full of powders and pills. He remembers more or less to the day when both the substances and the sounds changed and thus, quite suddenly (and magically so it seemed back then), the crowd did too. Walking towards the usual tent one night, only to find—in amongst the expected drunken and bedraggled crew—city kids, dressed in trainers and cagouls, dancing in a trance to the sound of repetitive beats.

John is marked by tattoos of different kinds. A record of the different places he has been and the various encounters he has had. Most are crude. Stick and poke sketches. All of them, grasped all at once, constitute a script of sorts to be read (but then we need to ask, by whom?). But there are also vaguer lines—and stranger figures— on his front and back. Perhaps it's a map of sorts that has been collectively penned for some other purpose?

Stripped to his waist now and kicking up dust as he stamps his feet, arms and hands moving in time to the bleeps and beats, eyes looking straight ahead and unfocussed, fingers coiling in tight concentric circles. All this marking out something in the warm night air. Something is being wordlessly communicated to those others around him, including those huddled together on the quarry top and, perhaps, others too that are further afield. And then, so it always seems to John (but only after the event), this message is also for a wider outside, for the hill above this quarry and for the landscape that surrounds this place. Even, why not, for the stars above. John feels he is at some kind of apex here, everything arranged specifically around him (and for him) as if radiating up and out from this dance that is also a still point.

And why do they call him *King* John? Is it only because he is always there, in the centre of things, when the tarpaulin is pulled tight and the sound system set up? Is it because some of the younger folk look to him (although, to be honest, this is often because of what he might have up his sleeves, so to speak)? In part, this is indeed the case. He holds a certain middle ground, and, with that, gathers and binds the rest. There is, however, something else, something deeper to this name of his. John seems to those who know him well to be a part of this landscape that he and they move through. It's as if he is himself something much older than his years. A remnant of something lost long ago that is reactivated by that other more recent device when it starts up its racket. And when this happens—so it often seems to those around him—then other things begin to foreground themselves.

Suddenly John's reveries are interrupted by a single sharp call. Not quite an animal, but certainly not a human voice. It's a bark of sorts that seems to come from some other place. It's a sound that reminds him of things left undone and of how things once were (and, why not, might be again?). And now it has been heard John stirs, gets up and begins to pack up his things and lock up his truck, careful in particular to wrap that heavy silver orb that has been his lot to carry all these years. Something summons him back and perhaps, he thinks, the others too? Only one way to find out.

*

What does King John bring to this set-up? That very much remains to be seen. At the moment he represents a decision that has been made to live a certain way. And, with that, also a way of life intimately connected to the landscape he moves through. John is also a somewhat tragic figure, residue of a counterculture now gone. Like the others then, he is partly a reminder of something already lost. He is also himself somewhat a broken man or let's just say he carries some scars that go deep.

Chapter 5: An Intervention

The four of them are variously standing and sitting around a small campfire in a clearing in some wood on a damp but bright morning. They have come together for an impromptu meeting to discuss what happened the night before and—not for the first time—what to do about Ribbonhead's drinking. Fox-Owl has called them all together, but they would have been here anyway. Where else is there to go?

John is the first to speak. 'There is no way—*no way*—I'm going to play opposite that drunk again.' He nods at Ribbonhead. 'Full stop.' 'That's the last time that's going to happen. Or, at least, the last time I'm going to be involved in this shambles.'

Silence.

Eventually, Hare speaks, stuttering and stammering out his words. 'It t-t-takes t-t-two t-to t-tango J-John…and, more particularly, the p-p-pot calling the k-kettle b-b-black springs to mind on this occasion.'

More silence. John's glare fills the space between them all.

Fox-Owl nods slightly, and then, after a letting out his breath (he had been holding it in whilst the above exchange took place) attempts to initiate some discussion on the matter in hand. 'Look, we're going to have to do this again. We all know that.' He looks, quickly, at each of them in turn. 'And, like it or not, there's no one here—as far as I can see—that can take on his part. At least not without some risk of everything coming undone.' He pauses, then continues. 'We need a plan—a way for us to move forwards with this—and we need to decide on it here and now.' Fox-Owl gestures in the air with his finger as he says these last words.

Ribbonhead stirs then reaches deep into his inside jacket pocket. He pulls out a tattered pouch. His hands are shaking as he attempts to roll a cigarette with some crumbs of tobacco and damp papers.

'Look at him' says John. The rest of them turn to look at their companion sitting hunched up on the wet grass. 'For Christ's sake someone give him a bloody drink so at least he can contribute.'

No one moves or does anything for a short while. Then Hare turns, reaches into his bag and, silently, passes Ribbonhead a can. Ribbonhead looks up briefly at Hare—their eyes meet and something passes between the two of them—he takes the can, opens it, and takes a swig.

'That is not the solution I had in mind' says Fox-Owl somewhat despondently.

After another pause, he continues. 'Any switching of roles at this stage seems out of the question. We all know there's a problem.' He turns to look pointedly at Ribbonhead. 'You know we know there's a problem. We know you know that we know there's a problem. Everyone knows about the problem that we all have. We've all been here many *many* times before. Let's face the facts. You will not—or cannot—stop drinking. And, as per usual, it's affecting how things progress. In fact, I think it's safe to say, it's getting worse.'

Ribbonhead takes another swig, then a drag on the thin and drooping cigarette he has managed to light. Finally, he speaks—or mumbles anyway—hungover and tired, but with the alcohol providing at least a flicker of inspiration.

'It's the only way I can see.'

Hare twitches, then nods quickly and strokes the back of his neck. He understands. Both the reason given and the tragedy of it all. Indeed, he has his own complicated history with various substances.

In fact, the truth of it is that all of them here have this history— in one form or another—and it is this, at least partly, that brings them together. Both the sadness and loss invariably involved on the way, but also—and as part of that—the sense that each of them has seen something. Been somewhere else. They are, as each of them grasps in their own way, a community of sorts. And, as such, there is a shared sense of purpose to follow this pattern that has, as it were, been revealed to them (at least at times) and, with that, pursue this other thing that often feels nearly within their grasp.

Who knows, perhaps when they see it again it will take them all with it?

Hare speaks quickly, furtively glancing around the faces gathered there as he does so. 'We need t-t-o use this, t-to t-t-t–turn things around, t-t-to make what is bad in t-to something good. There is something in all this. Something for each of us here.' Hare looks at Ribbonhead. 'He walks c-c-closer to that line than us other three. He is at the edge.' Hare picks up a stick and points to the ground in front of them all.

'This is where the work is. Not just on that stage.'

Again, the Silence.

As usual Hare has hit upon something. A truth about who they all are and what they are doing here together. It's why Hare's presence is essential. Ribbonhead is not a problem to be solved—at least, not on the level of interventions and discussion. Each of them, even John, knows this. They need Ribbonhead's sight. At least, until something else makes itself known.

Fox-Owl looks at the spot Hare is pointing to, then at each of his companions in turn. He is not their leader—none of them could really lead, or, indeed, be led—but here and now, he is certainly the one who has the most clarity about what needs to happen in order that things can move on. So that those few things of theirs can be packed away, and, with that, the caravan can travel to its next appointed place and, there, wherever it is, they can try again.

'I have a bold suggestion then. How about we—that is to say you,' Fox-Owl looks at Ribbonhead, 'agree on some parameters? No drinking immediately before the performance, which, let's say, means, at minimum up to two hours before. How would that be?'

More silence. Ribbonhead gives a resigned shrug and lets out a long sigh.

'I'll try.'

But even as he says these words he knows—as do each of them gathered there—that this suggestion, mild as it seems, will take an effort that he is almost certainly not capable of and that even if managed the toll this abstinence would take—on his mood—would mean any kind of channelling let alone performance would be impossible.

John speaks again. He has calmed down—a little—and his words are less harsh, more reflective, or at least resigned: 'Look, I don't know how much all of this is working out. It's been more or less alright these last years—but we're older now. To be honest, I don't feel too good.' He looks down at his hands then up and around at the rest of them. 'All of us look all bust up. It's less easy to get any distance or come into a productive relationship with what this is all about. Sometimes it all just seems so bloody pointless. I don't recall laughing much, even at the funny bits. I mean, like we used to.'

All of them are staring into the embers of the fire now and, with that, are remembering how it was. How they met and those first days of working out their parts. There was a sense back then that they saw in each other different set-ups but also ways out of whatever set-up they had found themselves in. Each had also operated as a point of inspiration (and often a point of collapse, it's true) for the others. Their parts, back then, had come easily. At any rate there had been no squabbling when that old painted wooden chest of masks and props had been delivered and opened up.

Hare speaks again, but this time there is less stammering and, indeed, a surprising conviction to his tone (though also some odd affectations). It is Hare speaking, but for a moment it is also as if something else is speaking through him.

'Step forward which of you here thought this was to be the easy ride? We knew there would be challenges. It's why we signed up. The hard stone wall was what we sought, not some jolly dance. So, Ribbonhead makes a move to escape what is rightly his. Again, step forward who here does not also try to avoid that which is their own business time and time again?'

The others are used to Hare's occasional change in tone—as if another actor had taken on the part—and, of course, none of them steps forward or says anything. All of them continue to stare into the fire. Hare continues, but now the stammering is back.

'There will be a set-up and a d-d-diagram. A particular arrangement that will prevent this re-o-c-c-curring. We need not only to remove the substance, but to change the c-c-context and the c-c-conditions.' Hare pauses as if for dramatic effect. 'I have myself a radical suggestion to make. For the next performance Ribbonhead plays the part of king, with you John taking on his role as pole and centre point. It is a part you could easily play.'

The last sentence is directed at John and said in a hopeful questioning manner. John looks up and jerks his body back. He is visibly shocked. 'There is no way—*no way*—that I will give up my crown. There is no one else that could carry this burden, at least, not here.' He looks around at the others. 'Perhaps, in another place and at another time, he might have worn such a crest.' John wags his finger at Ribbonhead. 'But it is way too heavy for him as he is now. His time, if he ever had one, is most certainly up.'

All of them look towards Ribbonhead whose head is bowed once more. The faded ribbons covering his head fall limply to the ground. It's as if he's not there with them, but in some other place they cannot reach. Somewhere far far away. A glowing log in the fire collapses sending up a small shower of sparks. From somewhere nearby, a single crow caws.

There is a sense of resignation in the air—a stillness and a sadness—but also a certain satisfaction that all this has been aired once more.

Even perhaps that this is all part of the script?

*

The four of them work quickly and quietly at their tasks—apart from various grunts and the odd sigh—each attending to their own few things whilst also taking care of the camp such as it is.

For Hare the packing up is always a hopeful time. A looking forward to the next place and a chance to move away from what, inevitably, disappoints (Hare is never satisfied with the part he has played, to say nothing of the other crises that invariably occur). He rolls up his sleeping bag, puts his small knife carefully back in its sheath, and that back in his bag. He takes the small wooden figure of a hare and wraps it carefully in a rag before placing it next to the knife. In Hare's head there is a song of sorts, or, at least, there is a kind of muttering and murmuring as he goes about his business— something to orientate him (if not to keep him together) in this morning routine.

John is restless and, like Hare, ready to be off. He is tired of this place and keen to move away from the memories of the night before. As with the rest of them he travels light. An old thin sleeping bag, two tattered polythene bags with a few things, though nothing of any particular value or that reminds him of any life before, except that silver orb he carries like a dark secret wrapped up in a cloth. Like Hare—like all of them—John desires connection. He feels this sharply this cold morning (old wounds are, indeed, resurfacing), although most of what he does—including his interactions with the other three—moves him in the opposite direction. He goes about his morning preparations with a deep frown on his brow and a grey cloud that follows him alone.

Fox-Owl—the most organised of a disorganised troupe—folds and packs his own things neatly in his small, battered suitcase. He then attends further to the camp, putting bags and boxes in the back of the cart and securing the canvas awning, feeding their old nag of a horse, retrieving the left-overs from breakfast and seeing to the pots, pans and plates.

And as he works, he also has an interior monologue going. A series of questions about Ribbonhead, the drink and the play. And how the journey is taking its toll on all of them. And then also there are other questions about what the point of all this is. Why him, why here, why now? Could not someone else have taken up his part? Operated as compass for this awkward band that roams the land, setting up each week or so for, well, a what? A kind of play but one in which no one can ever know in advance what will befall. Were there always things such as this? He suspects there were, though now perhaps they are less common. In fact, perhaps it is the case, he thinks, that such a set-up as they perform is summoned whenever it is needed, when other senses—and sources—of meaning have all been haemorrhaged out. And that, once activated, this device—if it can be called as such—then speaks to all those other pasts and future times. All those other places when other travellers have stopped and pitched their camps, cleared the bracken or fern, ready for whatever then would take place. Indeed, thinks Fox-Owl, there have no doubt been others who have worn his own creaturely mask—or something similar—and there will be others to come. In fact, he has once seen them all in a line, the same but different, backwards and forwards they came, as if called, when, once, way back, it was his time to take a turn in the centre of the round.

Ribbonhead is the last to move from the morning fire. He sighs, stretches his arms and sore shoulders, and eventually gets up and goes back to where he had slept. He picks up an old blanket and worn-out mat and looks around for anything else that might be his. Finding nothing he rolls his bedding and ties it with a piece of string he finds nearby. In Ribbonhead's hidden head there is a dullness, but also—through the fog—he is thinking back to yesterday's performance and attempting to understand where he went and what passed through him (although he is never sure that understanding is *really* what is at stake). There is a sense that something important occurred. He feels it in his body—something besides the hangover—something different did indeed come to pass. But what was it that he saw? Staring at the trees that fringe the camp an image suddenly comes to him. He sees himself as if from outside and slightly above. There, sitting cross legged in the driving rain. It's the dead of night and he is surrounded by the other three who are watching him close and, could it be, he is fashioning something quickly with his hands, his fingers twisting and kneading some material whilst the others look on. Then all of a sudden, he lets this bundle go. A thin stick-like figure, that has something of the hare about them. One foot in height, newly born. It looks at him, opens its mouth as if to speak but no sound comes. Then it turns and off it runs at pace away from the camp and into the trees. Ribbonhead shrugs. He does not understand that vision at all. No surprises there. This is often the case—although it is also sometimes the case that such visions are understood retrospectively. Eventually he gets up and goes to look for Hare.

It has indeed been raining hard in the night and a little later the large wooden wheels of their cart need some help to get them out of the deep muddy ruts. John, grunting, shoulders the rim of the wheel that is most stuck whilst the others push from the back, and soon, with each of them spattered in mud, they are back on track and heading for the horizon and, with that, a new place to set up and try again.

36

Chapter 6: On the Road

It's a long march to the next place—six days in all—with stops each evening on the way at a clearing in a wood or sometimes at the side of the road. Each time the tarpaulin is once again unfurled and beds—such as they are—laid out. Food is foraged along the way—unless some animal is found already dead—supplemented, here and there, by a gift from a thankful villager (but then, we need to ask, thankful for *what*?) or barter from a farmer's harvest (although this particular band of travellers has very little to barter with). All the talk—such as it is—goes around and around the same questions. What was it that Ribbonhead saw that night? Who was he when he took on that part (or when that part took on him)? And will whatever it was visit again? Perhaps even take each of them by the hand and, more gently this time, lead them to that other place?

An image then of four sodden figures trudging across a landscape, long shadows cast behind them by a setting sun. And with them a covered cart, pulled slowly along by an old, tired horse. On their way to different sites where, for reasons that are never entirely clear, there is sometimes a passageway to an outside of all this.

Fox-Owl has a map of these special places at which they enact the same performance (or nearly so). A repetition of all those performances that have gone before and—certainly this is Fox-Owl's understanding—of all those that are yet to come. On an evening and after they have cooked a meal, he will get out this faded document, unfold its creases and lay it out flat before the rest of them. He will point to the various shapes and lines, explaining this and that in hushed tones, passing over the darker areas and the various shapes and shadows therein and, always at some point, gesturing to what looks like a drawing in the centre of some dark sun.

Does this map have its own story to tell? A narrative of some kind about where it's from and how it's been used? It certainly appears as if some of the destinations—and especially that central spot—have been rubbed nearly blank by many a touch, as if this map were itself once part of some other ritual or performance.

Fox-Owl looks intently at the darker regions as if trying to work out the geography there. He gestures, silently, towards the others with a pointed finger as if to say, 'we are definitely on the right track'. Hare looks up—pauses as if considering things—then nods. John shakes his head and grunts as Ribbonhead bends down to take a closer look.

*

At one pause for rest Hare comes back with mushrooms. They all gather to look at what he's found—they're all interested that's for sure—knowing Hare's ability to sometimes pick the right ones, but sometimes the wrong ones too. John carefully goes through them one by one, turning them gently in his large rough hands. He checks their tops and gills, nods, then moves his head from side to side, weighing up the risks. He grimaces slightly, and, finally, suggests it's 'worth a punt'. Hare sets about fetching water from a nearby brook, then lights a small fire and on goes the pot. Once it's boiled in go the mushrooms and the tea is made.

Half an hour or so later they glimpse a vivid blue in amongst the trunks. Walking further and there it is. A carpet of bluebells. The colour is otherworldly, too bright somehow in this landscape of browns and greens. And the smell. A sweet pungent aroma. It's nearly overpowering. The flowers are everywhere, as if they had been intentionally sprinkled in between the Oak trunks.

Suddenly Ribbonhead stops.

The fingers of one hand are stretched out in a gesture of surprise and alertness. Then, after a pause, he says: 'There's something here with us.' Another pause. 'Look! In the trees!'

'Not in the t-t-trees', says Hare. 'It *is* the t-t-trees.'

Hare is right. It's the trees that have come out to meet them. Laughing, leaves rustling, they are bending down their boughs as if to brush against the four traveller's heads.

Sunlight falls through their shimmering tops. All is light and movement. All is dancing.

'A good meeting, this!' laughs John, as he lets whatever it is out there in.

All of them have stopped walking now and stand as if figures in a landscape painting. All the different shades of green are surrounding and crowding in around them. There they are in this scene but they are also watching it as if from someplace else. Each listening intensely—so it seems—to something that is both inside and outside of them.

'Is this it?' asks Hare, his eyes wide.

John laughs again and, squeezes Hare's arm. 'It either is or isn't, but either way it's definitely something!'

And a further something is stirring, happening to and with Ribbonhead. No longer is he bent. His head, suddenly erect, is turning and tuning in, and now it seems is receiving some kind of transmission. His arms begin to move—up and down, up and down—and then his feet, then legs, begin to rock from side to side. It's an absurd crab-like dance that has them all in stitches. Indeed, Hare falls to the ground, so funny is this sight, like a parody of everything Ribbonhead has done before (and, perhaps—who knows?—a pre-view of what's to come). And yet it is also so very here and now. So fully in and of *this* moment! John, looks on, nodding, a broad grin slowly creeps across his face, then, quite suddenly he is laughing out loud. He's remembering. *This* is what it's about! *This* is why they journey as they do! Only Ribbonhead could be doing this here in this wood. Only he has it in him to deftly side-step like this and let this other fellow—whoever they might be—come through. And what a joy it is to see *him* again! And, with that, to get a sense of what he can do when he finds a willing host! The lightness of it all! John stamps his own feet now and with that begins to dance. An imitation of his companion. A homage even. His fingers now moving in circles, feet kicking up leaves and earth.

Then suddenly Ribbonhead stops dead still again. And, as if they are in some children's game, the other three stop too.

All is quiet except for the bird song and a gentle breeze that rustles the treetops.

Then Ribbonhead begins to move once more. Arms like windmills now, slowly at first, then going faster and faster. He turns on his heel, ribbons flying then furling around him. This is what it is! This is *who* he is! The trees are shaking in agreement and, it seems, affirmation. They are themselves relishing the sight of this being, here now, with them, part of what they also are. But in fact, there is no one here at all beneath these ribbons, although Ribbonhead is certainly being directed somehow. He is spinning around and making various gestures with both arms and legs as if involved in some strange comic semaphore. There is an intention at work here in this place—no doubt about that—but there is also nothing here that needs to be understood. And this thing that is now within them all moves and watches itself move (hence the humour, the laughter, the absurdity of it all).

And as John moves he remembers a time when he too danced like his companion. It would be in a quarry or in a crowded warehouse. He was younger then, body less battered and bruised, able to move more fluently and fluidly in and out of this other place. See him now, stripped to the waist once more, tattoos fresher, the patterns less dense. Fingers, once again, making the circles as his stamping feet send up those clouds of dust. Yes, he recognises where Ribbonhead is and the ability his companion has to move there and of course—this is Ribbonhead's specific gift—to take them all with him, if only for a time and, even if as here, only for a short trip.

Although not dancing Fox-Owl also makes his travels, guided by this sight of his dancing friend with ribbons fluttering around his head. In his own way he follows in Ribbonhead's wake, sees the trees talking, understands that it is, indeed, here, it is now. But for Fox-Owl, besides this hollowing out, other images come thick and fast. Images that show him his habits. How he has reacted to what has come his way, and, indeed, those things that will continue to seek him out. It is as if a series of cards are being quickly placed one after the other before his eyes. All of his history laid out so as to show him—to make it crystal clear—what he is and will become.

And with this it strikes him—as it has, he now recalls, many times before—that he has a choice. To follow those ribbons and begin to dance or to remain where he is, in a certain pattern which, after all, is not the worst that can happen (at least, this is what he tells himself every time after these visions have occurred). The worst is to have no pattern at all.

And finally, for Hare, still laughing, still on his back. This is everything he ever wants. It is as if at last, he has breathed out and, with that, returned back into the world. No longer stuttering and stammering. No longer the odd one out but finally, for a short time anyway, arrived home.

*

The next day they arrive at a ridge with a long view out over the downs. On a hill in front of them, perhaps three miles away, there is a giant figure outlined in white. It's human in shape and there's something in its hands—two poles or some other kind or props perhaps?—but these are too faint to be fully worked out. Where this figure stands, on a steep grassy slope, it gives the impression that it has either just emerged from the hill or is returning into it. Certainly, it's as if it's in an entrance way (and perhaps those poles are in fact simply the door edges?).

This chalk figure is as a sketch, although the white lines demarcating the body are bold enough. It's been made to be seen by walkers along the track, but there is also a sense that another perspective might be had by an eye that is much higher up. An eye that is, as it were hovering over the landscape as a skylark. It's one thing to be there on the downland grass and looking at this figure on the slope but something else altogether to be able to grasp this drawing from up above as a small figure within a larger landscape.

They have clambered up the hillside now and are sitting within the outline of that giant's head. Burnt grass and some small pieces of blackened wood suggest that others have come before and camped out here, drawn to marking their own presence on this hill. Fox-Owl is looking at Ribbonhead, John and Hare. He turns and looks out over the downs. And then his perspective shifts and it is as if he is looking down from up above on this scene of them there on that hill. What else are they, thinks Fox-Owl, than four further figures like this chalk one drawn in and on this landscape? They are also outlines demarcating an inside and outside at least for a short time.

On another hill top nearby Fox-Owl sees another white figure, this time a horse drawn against the green. Another representation then that seems to be a part of the landscape, but also apart from it. From this distance the horse gives the impression that it is galloping. As if it has been animated by the very landscape it has been etched on to. Indeed, listening now, Fox-Owl fancies that he can hear the whinnying and clip-clopping of those hooves as it moves across the grass. Unfocusing his eyes Fox-Owl sees a line that connects these two hill tops together and then other lines that connect both of those with other features between and further off— mounds and ridges and other clumps of trees. In a sudden vision he is flying above this terrain and looking down sees the whole landscape is connected up in a network of these lines that run between these points and places. It occurs to him then and there that many of the tracks they have been on follow these other lines but that there are others that are still more hidden.

It's easy to get lost in a landscape where everything is clamouring to foreground itself. Whatever that fiction is that sits atop, part of its job is to select and censor, to allow only some of this information through. But then, of course, it is also part of their job at this place and at this time to try on some different fictions, to see which other paths and tracks these other fictions might suggest and allow. It's no good—no good at all—just being caught on the one deep track. To always see what one has always already seen. To be able to take on another part, that's the trick. To act 'as if' seems key. To have an intention but also to sidestep all this so as let that other fiction through.

Fox-Owl gets out his map and lays it out on the forehead of this chalk giant, carefully smoothing out the creases once more. There it is, different terrains and features, some of it connected up by the lines he has drawn and in amongst it all other figures and animals—and then other creatures that are less easy to identify—

that are all in this landscape. Drawn on the hill tops and on the valley sides. And in the margins of his map there are his various workings out and other diagrams and drawings. Some of which double those on the map, but others that are more abstract or seem to be working out more complex ideas. And more than once there is a cone there, dissected by planes, each itself with other landscapes—suggested with just a few marks—and then also further lines and loops between the levels.

Fox-Owl turns his head from side to side as if weighing things up then folds the map once more and puts it back in its leather case and places that next to his chest. He pats the place he has stashed it then looks up and across the hills and valley beyond, gesturing with finger and a further turn of head to the others that it's time to go. And then they're off once more, following the chalk lines, before stepping out onto the turf to follow those other lines and tracks that are more obscure.

*

Waking up another morning and it seems that a mist has crept up in the night and now surrounds them all in the pink dawn. It partly hides the Oak trees that encircle their camp, giving the impression—at least to Hare who is often on the outlook for signs—that there has been a fire in the night which is still smouldering somewhere close. But the smell is not of wood smoke. It is of damp and the end of summer. The sky is blue and grey with clouds billowing slightly above the fog. The shapes all seem to reflect one another as if the whole scene is alive or has been painted and animated somehow.

Fox-Owl is already up and gathering materials to get a small fire going. As Hare watches from his mat, Fox-Owl puts together a small bundle of dry leaves and twigs then attempts to light it carefully with a match, cupping his hand to stop the light breeze that has started up from extinguishing the spark. The leaves and other kindling are a little damp from the fog and dew, and it takes Fox-Owl a while and more than a few matches—and a lot of blowing—to get a small flame going. John begins to stir, woken perhaps by the smell of wood smoke that is now in the air. He grunts and raises himself on one elbow looking also at Fox-Owl. It's still and quiet but for that light breeze that stirs the tops of the trees and rustles the leaves. The mist is slowly dissipating but wisps still hang around and about the wheels of their cart and hide the legs of their old nag of a horse who stands chewing grass a little way away.

Fox-Owl has got the fire going well now and has put on a couple of larger logs he's collected from the back of the cart. There's a good flame, with a hiss of drying wood and the crackle of burning twigs. Now he is busying himself with their old black kettle, filling water from an old can. Ribbonhead at last wakes from his slumbers with a start. He sits up as if an alarm has gone off, looks around at the others there and then lies down again with a sigh.

None of them seem in any rush to move up and out of the night's warmth. And Fox-Owl seems happy enough to be silently watched as he goes about sorting some mugs and bits and pieces to eat. The flames of the fire have died down now and there are just red and orange embers ready for the kettle, which Fox-Owl careful puts on. John is sitting up under his blanket and has rolled himself his morning cigarette. He doesn't look up but tosses the pouch of tobacco and papers over to Ribbonhead. John lights the roll-up with a match—then tosses them over too—and soon the smell of tobacco joins the smell of the woodsmoke and mist on this autumnal feeling morning. The kettle is whistling now and Fox-Owl reaches over and removes it with a rag. He carefully makes the tea. Then he goes to each of his companions in turn with a mug, as if this is some old and sacred ceremony. Each of them gives Fox-Owl a nod as they take their tea. No words are spoken. Indeed, it is as if there has been some agreement not to break that morning's spell. Or not until they've had their tea at any rate.

Chapter 7:

Further Props and Other Prompts

They follow the track over soft hills and down into nested valleys. Occasionally they have a view of the whole landscape, stretched out before them as if it's a diorama. The track is sometimes worn down, itself like a small valley. At other times there are overgrown hedges lining the route. It's an old path that's for sure, gouged out of the landscape by years of use. But then when on harder stone it's flat and straight, crossing the fields and dales, even at times with further large flagstones placed one after the other. At the side of the road are different plants and flowers. It's midsummer and there are Foxgloves peeking out of what might once have been a hedge. They're tall and full, the hoods open. Around the light pink flowers a bee is buzzing. They stop for a while and watch.

The sun is high and it's hot. Blue sky and the occasional wispy cloud. There's not much conversation along this track, although Fox-Owl occasionally sets forth.

'It would be easier if we did not have the cart, but then where would we keep the props and other bits and pieces required for our play?'

John grunts. 'The issue is not so much our vehicle as this bloody track. It's not fit for a cart like this or, I'd say, any kind of travelling show. Why could we not just take the other road that is more straight?'

'As I remarked this morning John—and many other morning too—the play we perform can only be improved by a few stresses and strains along the way. It involves some preparation and walking this track is precisely that or, at least, a part of that.'

Hare who has been walking silently up to this point, lost in thought, speaks up. 'Perhaps a story would help pass the time and ease the strain? Fox-Owl have you another narrative up your sleeve? Something that runs adjacent to our own and might parallel this rough track?'

Ribbonhead is trailing at the back behind the cart but hears Hare's request and strides more purposely up the line, then speaks. 'Yes, a story or some other script would work for me too. I could do with something to distract me from the aches and pain that this old track is foregrounding.'

There is a pause in the conversation as they stride along the track and then Fox-Owl speaks again. 'Very well, I have a story for you here.' He turns his head to look to either side of the track. 'Although there is less a linear narrative involved in this particular tale.' He turns his head to look back along the track. 'It is about a track much like this and a group such as we are. I'll tell it to you now.'

Fox Owl's story of 'The Trackway'

> In older times the landscape was criss-crossed by tracks like this one. They connected up different sites and communities too. Back then all the land was marked up. There were complex monuments and other ditches and henges made of white chalk and green turf with different routes between which many would take at different times of the year. At that time there was no sense of having this or that. Possessions, such as they were, were shared. If there was a leader, they would emerge because of their foresight and care and what might be called natural ability. At any rate this was how things were and had been for many a generation. It was a magical landscape aligned with the sun, moon and stars and other less material entities that we know less about, having lost much of that perspective that they had. It was into this world—if world it is—that travellers from across the sea came and exchanged ideas and other things. And in relation to this story I'm telling you now, there was one in particular, a man that although in looks was somewhat similar to those he

46

found himself among had something different about him, almost as if he was from a different story. His clothes too were dyed different colours and the tools he carried were of a different order. More finely made. Anyway, he was made welcome, as was the custom, even though he was more outlandish than some who had come that way. As was also their custom—and very fine tradition in my opinion—they shared bread and food and talked around the evening fire. Then, after some days and weeks, when they announced that it was time once again to get back on the track and journey to one or other of these important sites, our visitor had asked them where they were going and why. Having no recourse to representation they had suggested he come with them to see. And so, all of them had embarked upon a track—perhaps this very one— into the sun and towards some site within the landscape. But when they had arrived at that circle of stones, which was indeed, their intended destination, and began to conduct their ritual and so forth, the visitor had stepped aside and said something that surprised them. Something they could not completely comprehend, but the gist of which went something like this. 'I do not need to travel to these sites where an alignment or some other knowledge becomes possible. The reason being is that I carry the sky with me.' That last phrase was the confusing bit. And, at that, he reached into his bag and removed an object wrapped in an oiled animal skin. Laying it down gently and unwrapping it there for them all to see. There it was a flat disc of shining stone—metal in fact, but these people had not seen that before. And affixed to the surface were other shapes and forms, all of it making a pattern that did, indeed, approximate both the heavens and—so it seemed to those standing here—the very site they were on and the track they had followed. There was this object, shining, glinting in the evening sun, the

very double of the earth and stars and sun that was
below and above them there. They looked down at this
carefully made thing that had been transported to this
place by this stranger and that, as it were, was a picture
of the sky and land but also of the very cosmos itself.
Certainly, it implied a different perspective, one that
none of them had seen before, and which now they had
seen could not be unseen. This moment changed
everything or, at least, was the beginning of a change in
the whole nature and outlook of that people. But that's
another tale for another time and place. Let's leave this
one here with these people at this henge and at this
hinge as things move from what they were to what they
will become, as they cluster around this first
representation and picture of things that is itself within
a picture which is—if you'll allow me to step outside my
own frame—here within this story I tell to you. And,
who knows, perhaps there is a further story which is
writing me as I speak all this to you? And even—here's
a thought for you to mull over—writing you lot too as
you listen to my story and walk this track.

*

At one stop for a rest and a bite to eat, John takes down his bag. He reaches inside takes out a bundle he's been carrying with him all this time. It's wrapped in wool and sheep skin to keep it safe. Unwrapped now and there for all to see. A drum like object made of chalk, about half a foot in diameter then three quarters of that length in height. It has a slightly domed top—with a smaller flat dome on that—as if someone has carved a lid to it. It's smooth, except for various markings around the sides and a few on top. There are diagonal grooves that make up a chevron design and the occasional diamond shape too. But then at the front—the most surprising thing about this object—there are what looks like two eyebrows and raised dots for eyes (almost as if it this thing is also surprised). Hare looks at it and immediately thinks of a musical box he used to own. It's not exactly the same—that object was more modern, that's for sure—but there is something about the chevrons on the side of this ancient thing that reminds Hare of the small triangles that slid across on the top of that other box. At any rate, it's as if his memory of that other object now hangs in the air—the image of that box superimposing itself on this drum-like object of John's.

'It's looking for its siblings this one' John says as he nods at the drum. 'There's always more than one of these things around. Always a few.'

Fox-Owl has come over and is also now looking down at the drum that John has placed gently on the grass. It looks at home there, the white chalk against the green. A drum—small and compact—placed in a landscape.

'I hear that these things are often buried with a child, is that right John'? says Fox-Owl.

'Aye, that's correct. They're certainly there to look out for something—if that's a pair of eyes that is.' John gestures with his forehead to the drum.

'Yes', says Fox-Owl, 'and to my mind there's something of the container about them. I wonder what was—is—in them?'

'Well, they're not hollow—or the weight suggests not' says John. 'Maybe something in them, but you'd have to break it apart to get whatever it is out.'

'Maybe they're a representation of a pot?' suggests Fox-Owl.

'Or part of a larger thing?' says Hare who has also now come over to look at this small fragile thing on the ground. 'I don't mean they're a part of a larger monument exactly—more as if they are part of a performance or ritual. So less what they are and more what they do, if you get my meaning.'

'Yes', says Fox-Owl. 'We need to be careful not to bring our own interpretations to bear here. Maybe these things aren't objects at all? If indeed there were objects and subjects back then when this thing first arrived. At any rate your drum definitely means something John. It certainly took some work to make.' Fox-Owl walks around the drum. 'To me—and perhaps this is completely because of who and what I am—it appears to be a prop.' He gestures with a finger in the air. 'It wouldn't surprise me if, once found, drums like this might find a place in a further performance as Hare suggests.' Fox-Owl then looks again at the drum and strokes the tip of his mask as if it's his chin.

Ribbonhead is standing behind the other three and peering over Hare's shoulder.

'There's a sadness here.' Ribbonhead remarks. 'Something about the face but also maybe because they were buried. And by a child. They're for the dead that's for sure. Something to mark that passing over to the other side.'

'Well, that would fit with how the other remnants and residues we can see seem to mark out a space and landscape', says Fox-Owl. 'It makes sense that whatever else the people were or were not, the line between the living and the dead was still there—even if it was a little more porous.'

'They're a message to us from that other time', says Ribbonhead. 'They're future orientated objects. Placed in the ground and have now been found. Maybe, even, they're for us to use somehow?'

'I doubt that', says John with a grunt. 'I've been carrying this one around for a while now and it definitely doesn't feel like it's mine— or for anyone else in particular.' He gestures towards the drum with the toe of his boot. 'I'm just looking for a suitable place to put it down to be honest. It's small but has become a bit of a weight. It's almost as if it's a constant reminder of all the other burdens I have to carry.' He tries to say this lightly, but they all feel the weight.

'Well, says Fox-Owl, we have it now and so it's part of what we are about. Maybe we'll find another resting point for it or will be able ourselves to activate it in some manner. Maybe also it'll lead us to the others if they're around and about. If, as you say John, there's usually more than one, then one thing's for sure, this one is probably lonely.'

At this Hare lifts his head and looks at Fox-Owl as if he himself has been named. John kneels on the ground and lifts the drum onto the sheepskin, wraps it carefully, packing also in the wool. 'You're treating that like it's your child John' says Fox-Owl. 'I don't mean that as a criticism, just an observation. It's already pulling a gentleness out of you.'

'Aye, and it always makes me sad too. Like it's a little death.'

'Well', says Fox-Owl, 'maybe that's the thing. It is for each of us here something different but the same. Perhaps that's its function? To foreground something that is often hidden or necessarily obscured? Like I said before it seems to be a prop in that sense. It brings a world with it. And I don't just mean the past.'

'Placed in the ground and has now been found' says Hare.

John has got the drum back in his leather bag now and it's on his back. The four of them are still looking at the place where this object was and now is not. An absence and faint imprint there on the grass. Indeed, those feelings and memories summoned by it are not dissipating quite as quickly as did the early morning mist.

And turning back now towards the track it's as if they are surrounded by a further drum-like world or are themselves inside a drum. The landscape spread out before them, the dome of the sky and the sun. Off they trudge now around and about the marks and tracks of this other world. Perhaps they are moving towards some kind of centre? The sense is that they have seen something within this world which is another world itself. The drum if nothing else surely announces this.

*

Walking along the edge of an old field, Hare spots it in the grass just by the hedge. A long thin pole, made of wood, shaped and smoothed. He stops and stoops down to get a closer look. It's a little longer than his height, about the height of Ribbonhead he thinks, and there's something affixed to the top. Or, looking closer, perhaps not affixed but a larger knoll of wood that has been worked on. Hare reaches down, grasps the dark wood and lifts it up. It's definitely a head of some kind that has been fashioned at the top. It's been carved that's for sure, but clearly the knoll with three knots was already suggesting a face—at least of a kind. The whole head is slightly larger than his fist. The mouth—if that's what it is—is open. The eyes staring out blankly. Yes, whoever carved it would have seen the face already there, and then made just a few careful cuts to reveal it further. The wood of the staff has been polished by many a grip—it's certainly been well handled this thing. Hare's hands slide over the glassy service. Holding it upright now the polished top catches the sun and Hare can see further markings—lighter cuts diagonals and chevrons—have been incised onto some of the surface. In the sunlight it no longer looks like a face, but like some other kind of device.

'That's an interesting find' says Fox-Owl. 'Strange that it was there for you to pick up Hare.'

Hare looks up slightly puzzled. 'Any of us would have seen it' he says.

'Perhaps' says Fox-Owl. 'But the truth is you saw it and now there it is in your hand. It certainly seems as if it is for you. An indication of something perhaps.' Fox-Owl tilts his head to one side. Hare has the staff in both hands now and is turning it. It slides easily in his grip, and he turns it faster and faster, eventually spinning it so that the face at the top is blur. The others look on at this odd piece of theatre, entranced, at least for a moment, by Hare's actions.

Hare stops and they all stare at the pole.

John grunts. 'But what use is it on this path?' He shakes his head. 'It's too long to help with walking and will just increase our load.' Hare has since passed the staff to Ribbonhead who now holds it steady in one hand, tip firmly on the ground. It is indeed almost exactly Ribbonhead's height. The sun is high now and there is a long shadow behind Ribbonhead of a giant with a long stick marked out in darker hues against the ground. 'All you need now is a crown' says Fox-Owl. 'And perhaps a second pole', he adds as an afterthought. John frowns. 'Don't go tying any of your ribbons to the top of it now, we're not in any shape to start a dance.' Ribbonhead doesn't move. It is as if he is thinking something through or, perhaps, simply feeling. It's as if the stick is an antenna of some kind. At any rate it's clear that this particular object in this particular location is having an effect on all of them.

'It's strange', says Ribbonhead, 'but I've felt all this before. I mean, standing here holding this thing. Not exactly the same but something similar. The set-up is familiar.'

John grunts again. 'You were probably a tree in an earlier life.' Then he snorts.

Fox-Owl speaks again. 'Well, this is something to reflect on.' He gestures with a finger towards each of them in turn. 'These coincidences and resonances are always indicators of a kind.' He turns back to Ribbonhead. 'It's certainly worth standing a while there and letting these memories materialise, if they want to that is. After all, most of them are just waiting for the opportunity.'

Hare is watching Ribbonhead turn the pole in his two hands and then speaks. 'Yes, when I picked up that stick it was as if I had a slight electric shock to be honest. It's charged somehow—although I'm not sure with what and it's not metal but made of wood.'

Fox-Owl speaks. 'All it takes to make a prop is some attention and then, perhaps an alteration. Even simply to change the context.' He looks around the spot they are standing in, taking in the field and hedges, the occasional tree and bird in the sky. 'An object like this is clearly made so that something else might be performed. Ribbonhead, do you feel there is something else it's asking you to do or say?'

There is a pause before Ribbonhead steps back from the group to find some space. He shuffles his hands down the staff that he now holds at waist height, and then, gripping it towards the end, he begins to whirl it around his head as if it's a medieval mace or some such. The others, quite alarmed, step back as Ribbonhead begins whirling the staff at quite some speed. And then he's turning on the balls of his feet, the staff outstretched, ribbons furling around his head. It's like watching a spinning top. Faster and faster he goes in the sunshine, the whoosh of the staff through the air. The glint of the sun on his ribbons as they fly and furl around his head and body. And then he's stopped on his heel and let go. Arms and fingers outstretched. Up, up and away the staff goes like an arrow loosened from a bow, up further and further as if it's been shot by some mighty strength. They can see it marking out a huge parabola…and then, at the apex of its climb, it's still for a moment, before it begins its descent earthwards.

It's too far away to see where its landed, a couple of fields away at least, maybe more. Ribbonhead is looking out towards where the staff reached its high point before the fall—his legs still twisted, arms still slightly outstretched. John has his hand up to his eyes to shield them from the sun as he looks towards where the pole has been thrown. He drops the hand and turns back to look at his companion. A deep frown creases his forehead. Fox-Owl has already reached down to pick up his bag, which is now on his back. He nods a couple of times and then gestures that it's time to go. Hare is the last to leave that place, looking once more at the spot that he found that prop, thinking perhaps, why it wasn't himself that had thrown it in the way his friend had done. Eventually he also shrugs, hitches up his pack and follows the others as they trudge along that path.

*

They have left the fields and hedges behind now and striding over the heathered moor. It's late afternoon and they have been walking for many an hour. Ribbonhead stops all of a sudden and points to their feet.

'What's that you've found now', says John, looking at the heather and a patch of gorse. 'Bilberries?'

'No, not bilberries John. Look!' There in between the gorse and heather is a patch of rock, uncovered perhaps by some recent heather fire. It's smooth and grey, but with patches of lichen here and there, and then also clearly carved is a design of concentric circles and small indentations.

'Ah', says, Fox-Owl who has come over to take a look. 'A cup and ring stone. Well spotted Ribbonhead. Most are hidden from view, but I fancy, cover much of the stone underneath the heather here.'

Hare has also come over and is bent down on one knee. He is tracing the outlines of one of the circles with a finger. He then moves that finger to feel the indentation in the middle of it. 'It feels fresh, as if it's been done just the other day. A marking of sorts to show us the way?' Hare asks this expectantly and looks up at Fox-Owl and the others.

'Perhaps', says Fox-Owl. 'Certainly, these cup and rings appear at different points and seem to mark certain places and, why not, the passage also between them.' Fox-Owl points to what looks like a feint line that connects two of the cup and rings together. 'Yes, they seem to me to be precisely a sign on the way Hare.'

'But what do they mean?' asks Hare.

Ribbonhead has also knelt down on the rock for a closer look, but then gets up slowly and removes his boot. John looks on incredulously, eyebrows raised. Off comes the sock, then Ribbonhead inserts his heel into one of the indentations where it fits snug. Having performed this odd set of actions he then reaches down, takes off the other boot and sock and places his other heel a few feet away in a further indentation. Again, it fits. 'Well, this is a fine charade says' John. 'In fact, it's nigh on a heresy if you ask me.' Ribbonhead doesn't say anything, but he nods at Hare who, reaches over to pass his friend that staff or pole he had found the day before and which they had—with some trouble—retrieved from a hedge in a neighbouring field. Ribbonhead lifts it in his two hands, turns it slightly as if checking its weight and fit—and then brings it down gently in another of the holes, this one smaller, and just a few inches away from his left foot. It slots in as if the hole has been made for it.

There he is then, this tall lanky fellow, coloured ribbons slightly blowing in the light breeze. Behind him the curve of the moors, various trees on the horizon—perhaps that's a cairn or two there too? The sun is high and catches both the ribbons and that odd face-like lump at the top of the pole. All is vivid and bright. All feels correct as if Ribbonhead has felt himself into the right configuration somehow. No one speaks. Bright sun with that light breeze. All of them are as still as statues or as if a spell had been cast.

After a minute or so has passed, Ribbonhead visibly relaxes slightly and steps off the stone and back onto the bouncy heather. He hands the pole back to Hare with a nod, sits down and pulls on his socks and then those battered boots too.

'Well', says Fox-Owl, 'we seem to have found an answer—at least of sorts—to what these markings are for. Ribbonhead, can you tell us anything more?'

There's an affirmative grunt from that bundle sat on the gorse and then Ribbonhead speaks. 'Well, it just felt right. I just had this urge to have a go and put my feet there. Once I'd done that, well, the other hole—for the pole—just seemed obvious somehow. At any rate it all just seemed to fit alright.' John's eyebrows are no longer raised but his brow is creased once more. He doesn't like these kinds of things that are strange and that cannot really be understood. He especially doesn't like it when Ribbonhead himself carries on in this strange manner, as if he's channelling another being or something similar. He much prefers it when Ribbonhead is just drunk. That's easier for him to comprehend somehow (after all he knows the coordination points of that set-up pretty well himself).

'And did you see anything else when you were astride that stone my friend? Any other information you can pass on or impart?' asks Fox-Owl.

'Well, nothing that's clear, but I did have a sense that what I was doing others had been done before. As if I were just the latest in a long line of fellows doing this thing up on this moor. And then there was something else also I saw through my ribbons.' He pauses and looks out over the hill and towards the horizon. 'The moor looked as though it were itself marked. I felt that there were more of these markings out there. Lots more. That they were on nearly every surface. And that between them, also marked out were lines and trackways connecting them up. It was as if that grid were made apparent to me from that position standing there.' He pauses, then nods at Hare. 'The pole also was part of all this or brought it in to focus.' He nods again at Hare, pauses, then continues. 'And one more thing. It felt correct that you were witnessing all this. That this stance was not just for me but for you to see through me somehow. We were all part of this set-up.' John's frown deepens. 'And, with that, I had the sense that what we were doing was also correct. That these markings were indeed indications that others had passed this way and done all this in their own times—and that others would come and do it all again.'

The sun has moved across the sky now, almost as if much longer had passed since Ribbonhead had taken his place standing on top of that stone.

One by one, they stand up, hitch their bags back on their shoulders and move off.

Chapter 8: The Stones

Later, as they trudge along another moorland ridge, Hare spots them in the distance—down on the plane below—and points. John nods. 'That's them alright.' Twenty, maybe twenty-five standing stones, irregular in shape, set in a circle. The circumference is larger than they expected and, leading off towards the west, there is a faint line marking a path or track of sorts. It's dusk and the stones look brooding, as if waiting for something. To be activated perhaps—or to activate something else?

For each of our travellers these stones mean different things. For Hare they are as giant pins stuck into the pattern of the surrounding landscape. They are from a time long gone, made by hands more skilled and knowledgeable (certainly than his own). They are markers of this other time and indications of another way of life that is now lost. For Hare there is a ghostly presence and a sadness round and about these stones. Even a kind of grief.

For John a henge like this brings memories—and images—of happier days. Of journeys on the road with that other caravan and another band of travellers. And, with that, a sense of belonging and connection to another community and to the land itself. These sites, back then, were places of gathering and exchange. Places of friendship. And later it was in places like this that a different technology allowed something else to transpire. It would be in a circle like this that tents and sound systems would be set up. Three days and nights of rave with all that brings. It was something like this—as far as John was concerned—that these stones were for.

For Fox-Owl the circle of stones—not unlike himself—were a fiction and a performance, though, granted, of a more permanent kind. They represented, above all else, human intervention within something non-human. Nature needed this attention and intention, it seemed to him, this marking up, for it, well, to signify. And it was also this that made the stones the perfect set-up and platform for a fiction within a fiction. A doubling and a nesting which, at times (he had seen it happen) would allow a questioning and a throwing into relief of that other so-called reality. The stones were themselves a device that could bring other perspectives into play.

Ribbonhead's take on the matter was, as always, clouded by other desires. Certainly, he recognises the stones as significant. In his own previous adventures, others like them had played their part. Like Fox-Owl, he understands them as both prop and platform (was that not also the case with the ribbons on his head?). Like John he had been to many a gathering at sites like these. Indeed, for a time, seeing Ribbonhead dance in the circle, or slumped against a stone, was a sign that something had begun or was coming to an end. And like Hare he detected something else, something different, at places like these. There was something in him that resonated with something that hung around and about these sites. If he could just get himself out of the way then this thing, if thing it was, might then itself get up, orientate itself and align itself with them all.

After a pause then—there they are once more, the four of them together looking out at that horizon—the caravan continues on its way along what now appears as if it was probably the main track towards the site. Certainly, they walk along what is increasingly a ditch, on each side a small mound of grass to guide the way.

As they get closer the stones take on more detail. Each is rough in outline and unique, as singular as any living breathing individual. Some have been shaped, at least a little, others simply placed, or partly buried, turned on edge or left in the manner they were found. Up close now it seems that all have markings (although these are half hidden beneath green moss and yellow and brown lichens). There are some natural holes and scrapes but also, some of the marks look as if they have been made by human hand—as if the stones, now and then, were themselves pages to be written on.

There is an intention at work here—who could mistake that?— but it is one that is impossible to fathom or reconstruct. Hence the way these stones are always upright and ready for re-interpretation. All that is certain about them is they have been moved by something—part of the landscape that's for sure (and, of course, of stone), but different in kind to a hill or wood. If nothing else these stones are evidence of a minimal alteration—even a diversion of sorts—and, as such, are the tip of what later will become a technology pitched against the world.

Enough abstract reflection. Ribbonhead decides it's time to celebrate their arrival and, reaching into his jacket, takes out a can that Hare had found for him on the way. He opens it, takes a deep swig and collapses down on his backside, leaning heavily against one of the larger stones. The others begin to unpack the gear, demarcating a further circle within this circle for the camp. Hare takes a bundle of wood from the caravan and busies himself with a fire. There is a fresh pit here, suggesting that once again they are not the only ones attracted to this place in these times. Fox-Owl then walks the site—John goes with him—noting the position of each of the stones, touching some, running his hands over ridge and hole. Feeling also the cold and the damp from the dew. And then at others he simply stands, straining, as if waiting for the stones to speak or, perhaps, tuning in to some other communication that is being made. For Fox-Owl it is important to get to know each of these individual sentinels—and the journey, as always, has focussed his senses—so that they might make their own mark here. It's important that things are set up carefully so that there is at least a firm foundation, a proper platform, for what might then take place. One thing's for sure, he reflects as he makes his rounds, they have arrived at a suitable place and are nearly ready to try things out once more.

Part II

Lights in the Sky

Chapter 9: The Poles

Hare is running along a coastal path. It's dark, but not so dark that shapes and forms cannot be made out. The sea and long wide beach are down a slight incline to his left and then there are dunes and scrub land to his right. He can already see them up ahead. Two giant poles, perhaps thirty or forty feet high and the diameter of a mature tree. They are a few yards apart, the nearest just set back from the path, the second set deeper in the scrub. And atop of each one there is the outline of a large triangle in painted wood. On the first pole it's the right way up—the tip points upwards—but on the second its inverted. Hare pauses his run to look at the poles. Their size and placing, the symbols that stare out from the shore towards the sea. All of it suggests an intention that is nevertheless unclear.

Then Hare realises that they are meant to be seen from the sea. He shifts his perspective as if to see them from out there. From a ship heading home perhaps? It doesn't look as if there are rocks on this part of the coast—both sea and beach are flat—but now he sees it, yes, it's clear. They are signs to be read from out there. They speak a code that is not necessarily known—perhaps cannot be known?—to those who dwell on the land.

Hare reaches the first post and reaches out to touch it. The roughness of the wood suggests the poles are old and have been transmitting their message for many a year. He can just clasp his wrists as he reaches around the width. These poles could only have been put here by giants, Hare surmises.

The wind is getting up now and whipping his clothes around him. Distant stars are becoming visible in the night sky. No doubt about it, these poles are meaningful. But any meaning is difficult to fathom, at least by this particular figure who now crouches by the base of this first post to escape the wind.

Hare remembers another coastline, further north, when he saw another pole like these. This time stuck deep into the sand, though far up the beach and at some distance from the sea. Atop that dark stick was another shape, a flattened 'X' which, at the time, made no sense, though it had registered deeply enough that Hare had drawn a sketch later on a scrap of paper. That pole too had seemed out of place. But now remembering that pole, and seeing these two here, a larger pattern was emerging. A wider communication seemed to be at work across the edge of the land. These poles were like beacon fires, thought Hare, albeit always lit. Always transmitting their message—whatever that might be—from the coast out to the sea.

In a dream later that night Hare sees more poles at different places in the different coastal landscapes he has been and then some in less familiar coastal landscapes too. In each scene it's dusk and it's as if he is looking back at the poles from out at sea. On some of the poles it's unclear what sits at the top. There are different shapes, even possibly figures or other complex forms. But on four of them there are more of the wooden cut outs. Atop the first there is a shape like an 'H'. On the second, there is the triangle again. And then on the third an 'R' shape. Finally on a fourth pole an 'E'.

HARE.

Upon waking the dream lingers. Hare is used to the world speaking back. It's part of his illness—so he's been told—to see intentions and messages everywhere (but then, he sometimes reflects, is it healthy to just see the world as mute?). But these poles are less to do with his interpretation he thinks and more to do with something somewhere wanting to call out or, at least, trigger something. And, indeed, there has been quite some trouble taken to get their message across.

Hare gets out his notebook and draws the landscape from his dream with the four poles and letters atop. It's funny, thinks Hare, how putting all this down on paper seems to make all of it more real. And then, thinks Hare, looking down at the image he's drawn there, it's also *his* name that has been written *by him* on the page.

Hare remembers a long time ago another dream that held significance for him. Indeed, it was perhaps the most important of his youth. Another landscape with hills and moors. A lighter sky if he remembers the details correctly. And there placed on the hills or above them somehow, hovering almost, another communication. Another single word set out in relief.

LAND.

At the time this had felt like a directive and, indeed, thinking about it now, it had been these letters and this word that had worked to motivate Hare to move from the city (if only to ground himself). These letters in this configuration were a reminder—from himself to himself as it were—of the importance of being out and away. But the thing that really stuck for Hare was that this dream was not just of a landscape, but also of the landscape naming itself as such. A strange kind of doubling then. But then also, it had felt back then—as it did now on this other beach—it was as if this landscape were itself a kind of stage set and that these poles were part of that or indicating certain stage directions somehow.

Chapter 10: A Painted Face

Hare is applying face paints. Some yellow and blue around the eyes, then some bolder streaks thickly drawn in silver from both eyes down his cheeks and in a continuous line around his mouth. He looks in the mirror as the transformation occurs. He can hardly recognise the face that looks back. All is strange and obscured except the eyes, though even these are brighter now that the lines around them have been hidden, smoothed out by the paint.

He had taken to wearing the face paint outside the performances too. Not much, just a hint of the same bright colours. It wasn't exactly that he wanted to be seen wearing make-up or to put himself on display. Quite the contrary in fact. It was as if the application of the paint allowed him to be more anonymous. Or, at least, to be hidden behind this other face that was more vivid than his own. This also meant that his clothes and the other bits and pieces that he wore or held became more prop like. He was always costumed.

There was a time further back when this attempt at disguise had been accentuated. Living together in that old chapel as a performing troupe, sleeping on thin mattresses on that cold floor with the endless improvisations and other discussions, they had—at the end of the night—put all their clothes in the one large, wooded chest—and then each morning they'd select something new to put on. The only rule was that they could not wear the same outfit as the day before. The idea was that this would help them break certain habits, get more into that space where it was easier to improvise and, with that, take on another fiction.

For Hare, back then, it had been a liberation of sorts. He had let out a huge sigh of relief as first he took out that flowery shirt, then later, more hesitatingly, a skirt. It wasn't so much that he felt, at last, that he had found himself, more that he had had a realisation that there were other fictions out there that could be taken on and that these other fictions would allow other feelings and so forth to flow or to manifest themselves. Putting on a different set of clothes meant something more than just the mobilisation of other signifiers. It was as if the usual cause and effect sequencing was here reversed. No longer a self that was expressing itself, but expression—of different kinds—that then caused a self (or different selves)—to emerge. It was, it seemed to Hare, a magical business of surface effects rather than of any deep enquiry and, as such, all this doubled the method of the group itself and what it hoped to achieve by performing its plays (although that was a very loose description of what they put on). Certainly, all of them there were interested in the way in which a performance could be both light and comic—moving on and between surfaces—but also deadly serious and, yes, transformative too.

The make-up is done now, and Hare stands up and leaves the covered cart. It's quite a sight seeing this figure in face paint striding across this open field. He joins the others there, all of whom are wearing rag jackets and hold sticks with bells. From somewhere off stage some music starts up and the others begin an angular dance, stepping this way and that, occasionally coming close and clashing their sticks. And Hare is in an amongst all this. At times it seems as if Hare is trying to avoid being caught by the patterns and knots the other figures throw. At other times it's as if Hare is moving outside of all this, watching it transpire.

Then all of a sudden it all goes silent as if it's all about to tip over. One of the dancing figures there shouts out.

'Is there a painted face here?'

And, at that, Hare steps forth and bows his head.

'There is a painted face here and I am it!'

He stamps his foot and as if giving a sign the music starts up again, but this time louder and faster. Faster and faster it goes. It's almost too fast for the others to dance. And Hare is whirling around and around the group as all of them try—mostly in vain— to step in time to the tune. It's chaos. There's stumbling and some barging and Hare occasionally comes too close to one or two of the others. All of them are out of breath now, but Hare keeps going, though looking at his face there are beads of silver, blue and yellow sweat. The face paint is smearing and dripping down his face. It gives Hare the appearance of something quite grotesque but still made up, the running paint demarcating deeper lines and features. And then, looking again, it's as if another face is foregrounding itself there. It's still the same eyes, but a longer seemingly hooked or beak like nose and mouth huge and down turned. The corners of the eyes now have streaks coming down that make this face an abstract mask. A creature has arrived here, but it's not one you would find in any wood or field. No, this is something much rarer and more, well, odd. Looking again now as this face settles temporarily into its new gait, there is something of the owl in the huge, smudged circles around the eyes and then also the suggestion of a fox's pointed ears on either side of the face. It's certainly no longer a hare that is dancing here but some stranger hybrid form that was, perhaps, always there behind that hare waiting to step out.

Chapter 11: Getting Some Perspective

Sometimes it would feel to Hare that what they were doing together was somewhat a waste of time. There was, as it were, nothing to show for it. It could all feel so meaningless or trivial at any rate. But then, at other times, it would seem to Hare as if the four of them were part of something bigger. Or even as if that bigger thing was simply the group itself. At these times Hare would get the sense that each of them was somehow an instrument that was being used for some other more obscure purpose. Or even that they were each smaller parts of some larger device. The performances would sometimes allow a glimpse of all that. They would allow Hare to get a different kind of perspective.

*

When Hare is completely lost then sometimes the call of the others can bring him back. Often he forgets that this other path is open to him. That there is another way of being in the world besides the loneliness that he feels. It's certainly an effort to follow that call when it comes. The last thing Hare wants to do in that moment— when preoccupied by this or that symptom or sign (and with any narrative that follows this)—is turn to others and open up. But he has found that this is always the thing to do if he can manage it.

Often, it's just a word or two. 'How are you doing Hare?' Ribbonhead might ask whilst looking up from packing his stuff. Or maybe Fox-Owl will suggest they walk together for a while and, as he says casually, 'catch up'. Then, if Hare can indeed open up, sometimes the mist can lift and another landscape from within the one he normally walks can also open up.

It's about being held thinks Hare. Or simply trusting that he will be held. It's the trust that seems to be the key. Trust that the others all know their parts and, if need be, can help him with his. What else is there, thinks Hare sometimes?

*

Fox-Owl had grasped the method one day when walking back home from the pub. It was early evening and he had chanced upon a small performance happening on the village green. There was a travelling group of players who had set up there, pre-cursor, it often occurred to him, to his own sorry lot. Strangely, there was no one there witnessing that performance. It looked as if it had simply turned up—caravan and all—and begun its play. But watching it unfold Fox-Owl had had the uncanny sense that he was somehow part of the action or, at least, that the ground he walked on was part of the round that was being activated there. That play on the green—he could never quite recall the narrative—had prompted the thought that was also a feeling that his own being there and, indeed, his life up to that point was itself a performance and that he was himself a character that had been taken on (but by what? That was the question!).

Such a simple device, it would occur to Fox-Owl whenever he reflected on this moment—which was often—but so important in its implications. Indeed, he was still living out the implications of that particular event—and the particular perspective it had offered up—all these years later.

*

'A certain amount of self knowledge is certainly an important thing Hare.' Fox-Owl is walking and talking to Hare. 'To be able to see how your body and thoughts connect is crucial.' He pauses as if reflecting further on the truth of these words. 'It's partly why performance is such a good method.' Fox-Owl gestures with a finger as he makes this point. 'It allows you to see some of this in relief as it were or as if from the outside.' Another pause. After all— and as you have said yourself Hare—it's difficult to see it when you're in it.' Fox-Owl turns to look at Hare. 'A device of some kind is certainly needed I'd say.'

'It's like I *am* a device already', says Hare as he strokes the back of his neck. 'But one that's broken or not quite calibrated.' They walk a few more steps in silence. 'But then sometimes when I play my part it all fits together somehow.' Hare looks into the middle distance. 'As if it's only when it's seen as part of another set-up that it makes sense somehow.'

'It's a good way of putting what we do here Hare.' Fox-Owl nods a couple of times. 'It's about setting up a larger context or, perhaps, a different frame.' Fox-Owl gestures with his finger again. 'It's why I've always felt that it's repair work in many ways.' They go a little further. 'It's also why it's especially useful for those who, well, can feel, a little broken.' He pauses. 'At any rate you are an essential part of this particular configuration Hare—as are Ribbonhead and John—and, for that matter, me too.' They have both stopped now and are looking out along the track and the landscape ahead. 'As far as that goes it's *for* you and all of us on this road. We can't know exactly what we're doing, however. There aren't any blueprints or plans for what we're about. The principle has always been, make the device and then see what follows. And that device has always taken on different aspects depending, precisely, on the space and time it exists within and the different components that have been gathered—or have gathered themselves—to make it.'

*

Like Hare, Ribbonhead has a notebook in which he makes little sketches and the like. It's his way of orientating himself and getting some perspective on what they are about. Sometimes it's maps he draws, often of his dreams, mixed up with the features of the landscape or memories of the faces and places he's seen. On an evening he'll get it out and review some of the marks he's made. This process is reassuring as if once put down on paper these scenes and other details take on a different presence and an agency (much like when he looks back and remembers things, they always take on a more joyful and brighter tone).

Today he's drawn a picture of the four of them by a small lake. Caravan pulled up by some trees and their old nag munching some grass. He's got Hare there tending the fire, smoke rising up, then Fox-Owl peering out from behind the caravan. And himself and John, sat together on a fallen down tree trunk. Just a few crude marks—he's no artist that's for sure—but he's captured them there or at least captured something about them all.

Another time he had attempted to trace the track they're on and then plot out the points they seem to follow. A kind of map then that perhaps doubles that one Fox-Owl carries close to his chest. But Ribbonhead's map was more like a landscape in relief. There was the suggestion of peaks and valleys, clumps of trees and standing stones. Other henges and trackways and then also simply things that had foregrounded themselves along the way. An old oak here, a ruined barn there. A quarry and a chalk man. A standing stone. Not always in scale, but, for his purposes, accurate enough. And then mixed in with this there were other things that either had happened or he had imagined happening. Or perhaps they were simply signs and symptoms of what was going on for him at the time. A crude iron throne in amongst those hills. A circle in the landscape as if cleared for a play. And then there were drawings of various objects and props too. A pole and orb and bottle and other stranger things. And he'd drawn some animals and other creatures round and about. Certainly, there was a Hare and a Fox. And different flowers he'd conjured with just a few marks. Primroses, Bluebells, Foxgloves and the like. It was all somewhat crowded that's for sure, and, at times, hard to make out. He'd done the main landscape in one go, but over time had added bits here and there. Smudged and redrawn, added detail.

Another time he'd drawn a different landscape, but this time more stripped back. Again, not flat but contoured, and marked out with a blunt point those points at which they had performed. Then rising up from these marks he'd drawn cone like shapes, dissected by planes. And each plane had further features on it—even, possibly, the same as in that other landscape, but ever more concentrated as the cone reached down to its point. And then, perhaps the strangest thing of all, there were features or entities that reached between these levels. Figures that might or might not have been crude outlines of himself and his companions as if they were themselves floating above or moving between those planes.

A fourth and final drawing to mention here, of himself, John and Fox-Owl holding on to Hare. Their three heads together, cradling Hare's head below. And around and about these four figures, different knots and loops that seemed to diagram different arrangements of them together, each diagram suggesting one or other of them at the centre. It was as if he had drawn out some possible set-ups and perspectives. Just a few lines but enough to suggest these other configurations. Perhaps the drawings were themselves prompts for some further work that was to be undertaken? It wouldn't be the first time Ribbonhead had seen something that was to come or had, indeed, summoned that other thing forth.

Chapter 12: A Bottle of Beer

There is a long line of assorted vans and trucks parked up on the verge of a rough track that runs a few hundred yards from the stones. Some are more battered than others, but all of them have seen more than a few solstices. There is a smell of wood smoke from the stoves and cooking fires, and, occasionally, the sharp sweet smell of hash. It's a beautiful bright day, clear blue sky, white clouds drifting in a light breeze. All is glittering. Even the oldest engine shines.

By one of the trucks John is sat by his stove on an old camp chair. It's late morning and he already has a bottle of beer in his hand. There's a fierce but happy expression on his face.

Then, shambling along between the vehicles, lopsided and lanky, with a pole of some sort in one hand to steady himself, another figure is there. Scruffy dreadlocks like tattered ribbons run down his back. He occasionally stops at an open door. Ribbonhead is on the look out for something. A blim of hash perhaps? Or just a bite to eat? As he makes his way along the track it's almost as if he is dancing, although it's certainly not a graceful dance and more a jerky step. Inevitably he eventually arrives at John's truck.

'You got a drink John?'

'Not for you. Clear off.'

'That's no good John, I'm here for the duration. I'm good for a lend of a bottle.'

'No, you're not. You give nowt back you don't.'

'I will this time. Giro comes in end of week. I'll pay back double.'

'You won't cos you're not getting none.' John takes a swig from his bottle and looks away.

Everything is still for a moment. Ribbonhead, John, but also, it seems, the others that are around and about are also silent. There's just the grey wood smoke rising from the camp in that blue sky and the occasional caw of a crow.

'I've got something here you might want John. It's not to drink or eat, but maybe's it's good as an exchange.'

John turns back to look and raises an eyebrow.

'What could you possibly have that I might want eh?'

'It's a song John.'

John nearly spits out the beer that he's just swigged and snorts out loud.

'A song? You got to be kidding! That really is something else, even for you.'

'Nevertheless John, it's here for you. How abouts I sing it and then we'll see?'

Again, the stillness.

And then John shrugs and looks away once more.

Ribbonhead coughs and then begins to sing. His voice is rough and gravelly, the same west country twang as usual, but more sing song, or at least, there is a toing and froing and a tune of sorts. It's a song about life on the road, about the camps and the caravans. About the festivals and battles with the cops. And then there's something older in it too. It's about the stones down the track, but also the hills and valleys, the trees and the green fire that surrounds them all.

At first John just shakes his head and looks away. But slowly he is drawn back. His gaze becomes unfocussed as the words of the song drift around them both. A frown crosses his brow. And then, is that a tear in his eye?

Ribbonhead's song is about lost days and, let's face it, lost lives too along the way. It's a song about a way of life that both he and John had chosen, but which for both—as for all of them parked up here—is increasingly a hard option.

Ribbonhead finishes the song on an off key note. The different figures and landscapes are still there hanging in the air between them, doubling that other landscape that they are also in.

John looks at Ribbonhead who holds his gaze. He nods just a little, gets up from his chair and goes into the back of his truck. A moment later and he is standing close to Ribbonhead and, after a pause, silently passes him a freshly opened bottle of beer.

Something passes between the two of them, something more than the alcohol which is a medicine of sorts for both. The song has reminded them of an ancient bargain that they both have made—and, more than that, that they are both hewn out of the same stuff. Indeed, all the differences between them that just a short time ago that had meant so much, are suddenly less relevant or no longer in play.

Ribbonhead reaches out a shaky hand and takes hold of the bottle's neck. For a moment both of their hands are on the glass and once again something passes between them, this time not just the ancient bargain, but, with that, an acknowledgement of the same ancient curse. Both of them need this prop to help them make it through. Ribbonhead is a reminder to John of what he cannot but help turn away from. A secret shame that this figure seems to hold. But then at times like these it is as if some other intention takes over and he is able to turn towards that which he would rather avoid. And what follows then is never clear but it never fails to make a watery eye. It's as if both of them are part of something bigger or, at least, have a part to play in some larger device. The song has foregrounded all this. Allowed this other kind of communication and with that, this other series of gestures to take place.

Does Ribbonhead also feel all this? It's difficult to tell. The world he moves through is like John's but certainly the veil between the shown and the hidden is, for him, less heavy or well-drawn.

A crow caws again and there is laughter from another truck just down the way. The spell is broken. John nods, then shakes his head and lets out a heavy sigh as Ribbonhead, clasping his prize, hobbles away.

John watches for a short while taking deep swigs from the bottle as Ribbonhead winds his way back along the camp himself taking long deep drafts. Then, when he's almost out of site, John sees that Ribbonhead has turned the now empty bottle upside down and stuck it at the end of the pole he's been carrying. He spins the glass with one hand then holds the pole up high into the sky where the spinning bottle glints in the bright sun.

Chapter 13:
Preparations and Memories

They decide amongst themselves that they will perform in ten days' time. It doesn't take long to come to an agreement. A few muttered words, various nods. A thumbs up. It's more or less the usual wait and means each of them has some time to prepare.

For Hare it is simply—so it always seems at first—a matter of fasting, sitting and making the requisite offerings at the appropriate times. It's not just food that Hare abstains from. He also stays mute and, because of the rounds of rituals, only sleeps a few hours each night. When not putting things in place and focusing on what needs to be surrendered, Hare sits, still as a stone, eyes closed but watching. He sits like this for an hour at a time and all in all for perhaps ten hours a day (and, it must be said, often well into the night).

The first two days of this work are always the hardest. Tired eyes, aching limbs. Hunger nagging. There is a desire for something— anything—to fill the emptiness. But by day three those bodily needs have abated, leaving Hare lighter and better able to see the lay of the land. And, with that perspective, more able to receive whatever comes his way. This thing behind Hare, whatever it is, needs this discipline and careful programme so as to be able to do its own work. Some sits are very difficult (to put it mildly). Hare's body, like all of theirs, is no longer young. Joints and muscles are stiff and after half an hour or so either go to sleep or, sometimes, are in excruciating pain. But Hare holds fast through all of this chaos. He knows that this is part of the process and that there are no short cuts here. That without the pain there is nothing to work *with*.

The method is to watch how whomsoever it is that is here is blown around, this way and that. And then to further tune in to it all. To focus right down. To feel a way *into* this landscape. To attend closely to these gross sensations which, under this scrutiny—with interest, but no investment—begin, at last, to break down. They are, after all, only made by Hare and by his aversions.

What follows, for Hare at least, is an understanding written in his blood and bone of what he is. Nothing more than an ever-changing bundle of reactions. They go all the way down to a hard kernel that—so it always seems—is reluctant to release its grasp. Why would it? Hare always and eventually returns to this place and to this hard thing that, he has found, is also a wall. It is at this place that he thinks (if thinking adequately describes what happens here): this is real! It is here, looking down on this tight knot that he *sees* Hare—as if from outside and above—stripped and laid bare, alone, shivering on that cold hillside once more.

In all of this work an hour can seem longer than a day. There is often sweat on his forehead with the effort of not suddenly leaping up, or simply stretching out a limb so as to relieve some trapped nerve or other old ache that has re-surfaced. It's the hardest thing in the world to do. Harder than a ten-day hike. But then, all of a sudden, and quite without warning, something different can occur. As if somewhere else, somewhere deep down inside, another decision has been made (but not by Hare, that's for sure) and, for a while at least (though this measurement of time has less meaning here) everything is let go. Some other lever has been pulled that offers release. Then comes something intense. A pleasure, but of a different kind and one that is itself almost too much to bear. There is an effortless focus and a sweeping through of this shell which sits on this edge. A hollowing out of Hare's body which, here, becomes a kind of vessel, but not one that needs to be filled. Something of Hare seems to remain in all this, watching and feeling what's going on—or, at least, *something* watches and feels—but it is not that other Hare that is all wound up in that tight ball. What then is this other creature that is here and now? A fragile thing for sure, but also something as wide as the moor. If it is still Hare who sits on that hillside, it has its head up there amongst the stars.

And then sometimes, there is just the hillside and the stars. Or, at least, none of the usual chatter. Instead, there is simply an awareness. Of what? Of simply being aware. At these times there seems to be a bigger mystery at work. Something else is there with Hare or, perhaps, is there instead of Hare? A landscape for sure but without anyone seeing it.

A world experienced without habit or preference.

*

For Ribbonhead this time is always the hardest, with nothing in particular to engage him and no place nearby to buy or barter for drink. His addiction is further along the road than the others there. If there are fingers curled around something small then these have long since atrophied and now Ribbonhead is nearly nothing but this reactive mechanism and this thirst. But, as we have already seen, he has something else. An uncanny skill, at times, to side-step this whole arrangement, as if the very tightness, the very fixed sense of self that his addiction entails, allows a bit of room and the possibility of a kind of shift. Ribbonhead can at times seem to move quicker than those around him—the episode in the woods would be a case in point—but sometimes, depending on what substances he has mixed with his own, he is also slower and more slurred.

And sometimes he is quite still or, even, perhaps, not there at all.

Back in the day, in a crowded bar, with everyone jostling and clamouring to be heard—there would be Ribbonhead, the usual two carrier bags in his hands (holding his few possessions or, perhaps, just some food for the night ahead), wearing a tie and ill-fitting suit (the reason for which is anyone's guess), whilst the world carries on around him. Out of place and out of time. A still point. A kind of a pivot driven down and around which things then turn. In that place, at that time, his appearance would attract no undue attention—despite the stillness and the ribbons on his head (although perhaps that's part of this knack he has of being not quite there?). But for those who look to see this kind of thing, there it was. Something gentle and lost. Unreal but also very real. In the world but certainly not quite of it.

Here though, on this moor, there are no crowded bars. No throng in which to lose himself and thus—anonymously—go about his business. Here, at this time and place, Ribbonhead has a different part to play. When asked by Fox-Owl if he was up for the job he did not need to make any list to weigh up pros and cons. He had been waiting—although he didn't know it exactly—for just such an offer. Something to come down at him and with a twinkling eye and a massive hand move him to another context. He was up and ready the following morning—a fresh start!—joining Fox-Owl just before dawn to move the caravan out of the city. This would be it! There would be no more of all that which had determined his life to this point! Fox-Owl knew better. It was, in part at least, Ribbonhead's addictions that made him suitable for this particular role. He had the hunger but also the one-pointedness that was necessary for the task in hand. The absolute focus of the addict looking for the fix. Indeed, when on his chosen tipple, Fox-Owl could see something else, besides this bedraggled form. There would be something looking out of Ribbonhead's eyes for sure, but, as far as Fox-Owl was concerned, it was certainly not looking out from any interior space. That something else was, it seemed, from *much* further away. At these times, it seemed to Fox-Owl at least, that Ribbonhead would become a receptacle for this other thing to move through and—if it could be coaxed out then why not?—to speak. To tell them all about this other place it was from.

*

John had also known the kinds of places and spaces that Ribbonhead had lived in and through, though he had himself always preferred the open road to the cramped squat. Certainly, he had also had his fair share of drink and drugs and, for one reason or another, had side stepped the more usual narratives. He had once travelled with his own van in a convoy, beaten and battered but lovingly tendered to, tinkered with at various sites. A home, at least of sorts. Inside, at the back, a bed and old armchair, a stove with kettle and pan. Parking up—perhaps by some stones like these, why not?—back doors open to the setting sun. With friends sometimes but mostly alone. Kettle boiling, roll-up in hand. This, he felt back then, was truly the life.

But all good things must come to an end and John's life, like that of the many others around him, was brutally stopped by law and legislation. A battle in a field and, well, a change of direction in the wind. A lack of tolerance certainly, but this was not the real reason for that particular shift. Something more insidious had crept silently into the camps and caravans. Something far more dangerous than a cop with a stick. Something darker that announced to many of them that this life on the road, a life of not-doing, was no longer an option. And with that it was as if all the exits were increasingly being blocked.

John had seen Ribbonhead around. They frequented the same sites after all. But John had avoided him. It was as if that figure with the ribbons on his head represented something too much—or something too *accurate*—for John to approach. When the call had come—and things really had changed—it was as if he and Ribbonhead were the last two standing (or in Ribbonhead's case more slumped). There were still plenty of others around and about but let's just say they were mostly on their way to a somewhere else. And so began not exactly a friendship and not simply a rivalry. John's attitude to Ribbonhead was like his attitude to those parts of himself he did not like. Hence the ill temper, the impatience but also, at times, the sympathy and—although he might not admit it—the fascination with this figure that seemed to carry so much (or was that John's projection?). And yet, despite all that burden, this figure with the stupid ribbons on his head, could be so playful, so light and, indeed—John had seen it with his own eyes *many* a time—could, at times, channel something that John instinctively new held meaning for himself and for others. Thus, again, when Fox-Owl came knocking John not only heard, but more or less immediately heeded the call. Surprised—and yet not at all—that there, already, in the cart, was Ribbonhead, taking a slug from a newly opened can.

*

Fox-Owl wakes the first morning at the site, lifts his aching body off the bedroll and peers out of the canvas bender that has been his home for the night. The fire has gone out but is probably still warm enough, he thinks, to get going with a bit of work and then, well, make some tea. He's up just before the dawn which is how he likes these days of preparation to begin. Occasionally he will see Hare returning from one of his night-time journeys or, sitting still as a statue at the edge of the camp (if, indeed, it *is* Hare that is sitting there, Fox-Owl is never quite sure). But in either case each ignores the other, understanding that neither of them, at that time, wants conversation or even acknowledgement, focussed as they are on their own particular thing.

An hour later, and as the sky begins to turn pink, Fox-Owl sits by his morning fire, drinks his tea and reflects. He would never have expected (or wanted) a role such as this when, all those years ago, he had started—he forgets now what the prompt was—to make the mask he now wears as a matter of course. He had a short history in amateur dramatics it's true. He had performed in various village halls and, occasionally, on a village green. And he had certainly seen mummers before at those certain times of year. But it had never occurred to him—consciously at least—that this might be a path to follow. Or even a point of view around which to organise a life.

In the early days he had stayed up late and written scripts—or, at least, sketched out some protocols and parts—and, with some success, had attempted directing. And yet it soon become apparent that these attempts at writing were all unnecessary. There were, in fact, already more than enough fictions in the world, many of which had stood what they call—Fox-Owl smiles to himself in the dawn half-light—the test of time. He could simply adapt those stories with their various characters, their dialogue and other details. The trick—for trick it seemed—was not to worry too much about the specific fiction or about what might be said, but to follow it closely, to take it *seriously*, even if—especially if—this also meant going along with any comic tone. He had then forthwith set out to assemble his troupe. It wasn't hard. All it required was for him to go visit those overlooked places and seek out those figures with that mixture of lostness and focus in their eyes (a look that said they would be up for more or less any job that involved something different to what had come before). And, with each meeting, the shape of the particular fictions had solidified, the different parts come into focus.

As, indeed, had the darker places they would no doubt need to visit.

Fox-Owl had himself spent more than a little time down in that place beneath. In fact, for a while, he would make frequent trips—spending time, also, on the edge—checking himself, then sometimes checking in with others, before making the descent. Everyone, he had quickly learnt, had a shadow side. Some place they did not want to go, but which nevertheless called them down. Indeed, it was often the case that individuals would return even if—especially if—their journey had been full of pain.

From the outside then—or, let's just say, the upper world—Fox-Owl, like the rest of the group, cut a tragic (or, at least, a tragicomic) figure. Certainly, there was a bit of a limp and a stutter, more or less common traits amongst this band. And, with that, a not quite being able to communicate correctly, or with the right tone. Attempts at humour, too, would not quite hit the mark. Kind, one might have said. Yet, perhaps, not quite all there.

But then at those times when a descent is made and then here we all are in a place where nothing is secure—peopled by horrific figures, avatars and ghosts—something else about Fox-Owl would foreground itself. In that childhood landscape of dread—a place where it is all too easy to lose one's bearings, and, with that, to shout out in fright—it would be then, quick as lightning, that Fox-Owl would be in and at work, eloquent and immediate. Present and, it seemed, in his element. Just when the whole group would be beginning to tip and go off balance—threatening to collapse—there would be a look, a few words or a small gesture perhaps and with that the righting of the ship once more.

It was this that set him apart from others that did this work but then returned to another life. Fox-Owl made more sense when down below. He had spent so much time in that darker landscape that he was able to hold fast to whatever came out. A kind of strength then, but one that came from an extreme vulnerability—for certainly Fox-Owl had been to the very bottom of that pit—seen himself, small, unloved, abandoned and not retreated from that sight. And then, as if guided from some other centre that was only apparent *down there*, he had held out his hand to this, his former self. It was this skill, this ability to hold firm and also to navigate in and through this other place that meant he had been chosen—or had chosen himself?—for the task at hand.

Chapter 14: Lights in the Sky

The second night at the stones John has a vivid dream about a landscape. It's the kind that feels as if something essential has been foregrounded—about himself but, perhaps, the others too?—and which, as such, follows one into the waking world.

You are walking all alone on a hillside. A dark landscape of moors and woods surrounds you. There is a river and waterfall that falls into a deep dark pool. It's cold and raining hard. Next there is an image of something silver—an orb of sorts—at the bottom of that pool. Then, something terrible comes. A huge black shadow of some kind, flying through the air. It stops and hovers around and about. Watching and waiting. There is a sense that everything here is urgent, necessary and inevitable. And around all this—the setting but also, somehow, the overall atmosphere— there is a closeness and heaviness. On the river there is a small boat tethered to a small wooden jetty. In the boat is a figure in a black cloak or long coat and a large hat of some kind on their head. This figure turns slowly towards you. They have something of Fox-Owl about them, though the mask is both larger and darker. As they gesture to you to come on board, their movements are slow, as if they have been drugged (or is it that you have been? It's not clear). You walk along the jetty and step out and into the boat which rocks gently from side to side as you climb on board. It soon settles and then begins to move away from the bank. And now it's no longer a river but a broad lake or sea that the boat

*silently glides across. In the distance now there is a
darker line that suggests another shore up ahead. In no
time at all the boat reaches this other shore and your
ferryman gets out, wades through the surf, then pulls
the boat up onto the stones of the beach. They turn
towards you and point inland and now you see that in
fact this figure is not Fox-Owl at all but has dark
ribbons that fall across their face. You begin the walk,
looking out through what you realise now are eye holes.
You are yourself wearing some kind of mask or, it
seems, some large and uneven papier mâché head. It's
not heavy, but it is awkward and restricts the
movement of your neck. Up ahead there is a ridge of
sorts and a path going towards a cliff side which you
begin to climb. The wind is getting up now, blowing
your clothes against your skin, rocking this head that's
not yours—of this you're sure—but which is somehow
on your shoulders. You reach up with one hand to
steady it, the other hand reaching down to grasp clumps
of grass to steady your climb. You're nearly out of breath
but keep going. At the top now and it's flat with a clear
view ahead. There is a path that winds down and away
from the top, then across a broad and grassy plain. And
there, in the distance, you see it. A dark standing stone
perhaps twelve foot tall. You slowly begin the walk
along the path which is in fact nothing more than an
indentation in the grass. And as you go you think you
hear a sound. Something like a bell. Certainly a ringing
of sorts. At first you're not sure if it's coming from inside
this head you carry on your shoulders, but as it gets
louder it's clear that the sound is coming from outside
and from the direction of the stone. You stop to listen
and, within the sound, it's as if other sounds—voices
even?—are present but muffled or, at least, partly
obscured. The stone is perhaps a hundred yards away
now, and, looking through what is becoming dusk, you
fancy you can see a still figure standing by it. Someone*

*tall and dark who looks to be wearing a crown. And
with that you are suddenly lifted up and out of your
body and looking down and across at this scene laid out
before you. And what you see is this figure with the
dark crown and nearby someone else. Someone stooped
and stumbling along a path. On their shoulders is an
over-sized and mis-shaped head, crudely painted in
browns and black, with green and yellow streaks
coming from the eyes. It's a monstrous approximation
of what a hare or some other animal might be.*

*

The same night Hare also has an important dream about a Musical
Box.

*Hare is standing at the edge of a large lake under some
trees. There are others with him, Ribbonhead and John
and, he thinks, Fox-Owl—although the mask on that
third figure is larger and looks heavier, with features
distorted as if the rain had washed some of the paint
away (which is strange, Hare thinks from within the
dream, as Fox-Owl's mask is not painted). They are all
looking at another group sat with crossed legs under
one of the larger trees, eyes closed. All of these seated
figures are as still as the landscape they sit within. They
are also all dressed in clothes that have seen better days
and—so it seems to Hare within the dream—they are
concentrating hard. Next the scene shifts and Hare is in
a church of some kind, sat up in the chancery on what
seems to be a pew. Fox-Owl is next to him, and he can
see now is embroidering some kind of banner, stitching
also patches of cloth on to it. He can just about make
out the words of this needlework: THE ANCIENT
DEVICE. And then, behind these words as it were—a
backdrop within the backdrop—there is a landscape of
soft hills with clumps of trees atop. John and*

Ribbonhead are also there, looking directly in front to what is a kind of stage or, at least, a spot that has been cleared on the cold stone floor. And then, as he and they watch, a dragon of some kind appears in mid-air above the floor. Large and writhing and floating there, its silver and green coils twisting and turning, its mouth with fangs opening and closing silently. Fox-Owl looks up and then back down and continues his work but the others continue to look on. The dragon is not of this world, of that Hare is sure. It's more translucent somehow. But it is here now, summoned somehow for them to see. And now Hare realises that there are others sat on other pews also watching as this performance—if that's what it is—takes place. Hare now looks to the figures next to him—and to John especially who is here but younger, more present somehow with tattoos less dense. On his forearm there is a figure outlined in broad dark black line. A willowy thin creature, human in shape but with a large head, somehow shaped like a Hare (but out of proportion and monstrous). And then, on the other forearm, another figure, the same size, again, tall and thin, black ribbons covering a hidden face. Hare looks up and back to the front once more and the dragon is dissolving somehow. It's gone now and, in its place, again in mid-air and turning slowly around and around there is a box of sorts. On its sides it looks like painted scenes of different landscapes. The top is made of small triangles which, as he watches, slide apart and open as if some mechanism had been activated. And then, emerging from this box, itself slowly turning, there is another figure, small and still as if a model, painted in bright colours. It's Fox-Owl or, at least, a miniature version of him, standing there with map in hand, turning and turning until the mechanism stops and this figure looks straight ahead at the audience gathered there. There is a smattering of clapping, which then increases. A few cheers. And then

this figure begins to turn again—this time in reverse—
and slowly descends into the box before the mechanical
leaves do their work and close it up. Hare has the sense
in the dream that this display is showing him something
crucial, but its meaning is just beyond his grasp or just
out of range somehow (or it occurs to Hare, is not to be
interpreted in that manner but simply witnessed—or
looked over—a process which will then allow it to do its
work). It also occurs to Hare—watching all this
unfold—that he has a job to do, although, once again, it
is not entirely clear to him what this job actually is.
Fox-Owl has finished the banner now and him and
John have got up from their pew and are pinning the
banner up on the wall behind the performance space.
Looking again now, and the picture, flat against the
wall has become a window of sorts, with the
embroidered and patchwork features now an actual
landscape as if seen from afar. And there, in the air,
hovering as it were, is the box again, this time closed
and static. There is sense of waiting for something to
happen but—yet again—it's not clear what. And then,
with crystal clarity, Hare understands what it is he
needs to do and, with that there is a nearly
overwhelming sense of joy—a relief somehow but
overpowering as if he had taken a drug. Even in the
dream Hare feels all his aches and pains disappear and
a bright alertness take their place. He gets up and walks
towards the box that is there just above this landscape
and reaching out takes hold. But it is not his hand that
is doing the grasping; it's some other giant hand. With
this realisation it is as if he sees—or is (it's unclear)—a
giant hare, head in the clouds, looking down at this
performance that is taking place. And then there is the
box in his two hands, and he sees it has a handle as if it
were indeed some kind of musical box.
He turns it and the lid slides across again and then
from inside another figure emerges slowly turning as

Hare himself continues to turn the handle. But this time it is not Fox-Owl that emerges but Ribbonhead holding some kind of pole or staff—small and bright as if, again, a freshly painted figurine. Hare turns the handle again and Ribbonhead turns the other way and descends into the box. The lid closes, then—as Hare keeps turning—it slides open again and this time it's John, all shiny and new, gold crown upon his head and gold cloak across his back. More turning and finally it's the Fox-Owl figure that once more emerges from the box, small, black clothes and with that black and bright blue mask with the large eyes. Another turn and Fox-Owl descends. More turning and this time the dragon emerges. It's not static like the other figures but twisting and coiling. As Hare looks on it grows larger and larger until it obscures the box, then larger still so that Hare can see every detail, every scale, then even larger, filling up the whole sky.

*

The night before the performance something else visits the camp. Hare sees it first (he's up, as usual, doing his thing). He wakes Fox-Owl who has only just got to sleep. Both of them rouse a grumpy John, then, finally, they find Ribbonhead on his mat and who is particularly difficult to stir. Eventually all of them are standing on the dark moor, four small grey figures staring up at the vast night sky. And there, high above them, are shimmering lights, all different colours, dancing. They are so bright that they cast a shadow behind our four.

'It's a good omen', says Fox-Owl at last, though he does not sound absolutely sure about that.

'It's an omen, that's for sure', says John.

'They are v-v-visitors', says Hare. 'Come to b-b-bid us well on the eve of things.'

Ribbonhead, bleary-eyed, says nothing, but nods at Hare's words. Certainly, for him, these lights look familiar somehow (from a dream perhaps?). Over this landscape, in this particular night's sky, they appear both appropriate and out of place, although Ribbonhead would not use those words or make that analysis exactly. They represent a rupture or rent of sorts—not necessarily unwelcome—in how things more typically are.

'I've not seen anything quite like them before', says Fox-Owl. 'Although I've heard tales that lights like these can appear at the very edge of things. Not, usually, to those on the lookout though. Certainly, they are a visitation of sorts.'

'Aye, they don't belong here, that's for sure', says John, frowning.

'They might not b-b-be of this place but they are f-f-for us', says Hare. 'They relate to the t-t-task in hand—how c-c-can they not?— here they are and here we are looking at them. They and we are c-c-connected.'

'It would certainly seem as if this display is for something that watches from this particular point of view on this moor', says Fox-Owl. 'Although I'm not sure these lights are signs to be read. Perhaps, rather, they are triggers for something else? Or forerunners of a further thing?'

At these last words Ribbonhead looks up through that mess of faded fabric once more, and looks more carefully this time, and— could it be?—fancies he sees a face of sorts up there. Or, at least, two eyes, a nose and mouth demarcated by the lights. It might be an illusion, but this face, it seems to him, is watching them from far away. Surveying them as they survey it.

John, for his part, now also sees something else up there. A different landscape lit up by these lights and made by the clouds that are now building up in that once clear sharp sky. A landscape that doubles the one they are standing on. It seems like rolling hills have come in—with different peaks and valleys—and, could it be, in the centre, around where the lights dance, there is a black hole? Or at least a patch that is darker than the rest of the sky. A familiar coldness comes over John as fear begins to take hold. There is something about that place up there that he recognises. There is, up there, somewhere he does not want to go and yet, here he is, looking up and following these lights to where they seem to lead.

Although he does not tell the others—he's not sure why—Fox-Owl has seen lights like these before. Once, when younger—and before he made the decision to put on his mask and leave—he had been out alone on a different moor when lights like these had come, but much closer then. As close—if he remembers this rightly—as his hand held up in front of his face. On that night the lights had seemed at one point to pass right through him. And with that there had been a sense that his borders had collapsed and though he was there, he was also not there at all. He remembers looking down at himself in that strange luminous light and seeing his outline but not really recognising it. The strangest of experiences that he had buried for one reason or another and only now—seeing these lights again—recalled. Certainly, standing on that moor, there is an echo of that other night, for all at once he sees himself and the others next to him in outline only and as if from some other vantage point. Somewhere outside himself, or at least somehow *beside* himself and above this scene. And, once more, he could not quite see himself as part of that group, as actually there, but as, somehow, apart, separate from things, watching all this unfold.

For Hare these lights announce the arrival of something from far away but that for some reason has decided to make the journey and manifest for them here. These lights are a line thrown out to them at last and, with that, another communication of sorts. They are a demonstration that there was something else out there, something beyond their own particular life worlds with all that that implied. The lights were an opportunity, at least for a while, to step out of their current context. They offered up a wider perspective. Hare was certain they were an indication that they were all on the right track.

'A good sign, a good sign', says Hare, nodding quickly. 'There is no d-d-doubt we have arrived at a suitable place—and also that it is the appropriate t-t-time.'

'Well, it certainly makes a change that we have an audience watching us', remarks John. He tries to say it lightly but there is something behind the words. Something more serious and, well, a little scared.

'Yes', says Fox-Owl. 'We are being watched by something here tonight.'

Eventually the lights begin to fade back into the dark background from whence they came. And, similarly, each of our travellers, one by one, retreats like an inward breath, back to their particular place to sleep, or try to. All, that is, except Ribbonhead who remains alone on that moor. He seems now to be more awake and more alert. Certainly, he is standing more tall. There he is, once more a receiver of sorts, tuning in to some kind of transmission that the lights are merely the visible sign of. He is certainly attending to something. Turning things around just as, on this planet, at this time, there is a larger turning around some other centre far away. Eventually, however, even Ribbonhead retires to his sack, the signal now faded, and all is quiet and dark.

*

Later that night John has a second vivid dream that feels as if it is also a sequel to the first.

> *You are looking down from some point up above. The view is of a large village or town and there, down on the main street, there is a figure walking. They have ribbons coming out of a kind of hat or, at any rate, covering their face and they are striding with some purpose, but also as if to get somewhere without being noticed. And yet as they walk people stop their conversations, put down their shopping bags and turn to look. Nothing is said out loud but there is some tutting and the shaking of heads. It does not seem to be a surprise—to you or them—to see this figure here (perhaps this is their home?). More as if there is a sense of shame connected to them or walking with them there. The figure goes all the way past the houses and shops, through some surrounding fields and then climbs up onto the moors and, into a wood. Beside a large old fir tree, they kneel down on the ground, reach into their pocket and take out three small silver figures: a hare, a fox and a king sat on a throne. This other figure now*

*digs down with their other hand—as if making a
shallow grave of sorts—and lays the three objects in the
earth before covering them with the soil, then leaves
and twigs. They pause, as if reflecting or perhaps saying
something to themselves. And then up they get and
they're off. Out of the woods and up on to the very top
of the moor. It's up here that they find a tall painted
pole driven into the ground. From its knotted top hang
long ribbons, the double of those on their head. The air
is still and the ribbons hang limp. It's noon and the sun
is high in the sky. There are no shadows only brightness.
And at that moment you realise, of course, that this is
Ribbonhead (why did it take you so long?) and that you
are this figure, but at the same time you are also
looking on this scene as if from outside. You raise one
hand and brush some of the colours away from your
eyes so as to be able to look out over the landscape
below. Deep valleys and moorland hills lit up by the
sun. Then, turning around you see that there is a bird
of sorts also there. An owl, but human in size and with
a face like a fox. It looks at you with its large blue eyes,
ruffles its feathers, then gestures with its head to
something lying on the ground by its side. There, on the
heather, curled up, is a small baby, eyes closed, sleeping
peacefully. There is a charmed air about this scene as if
a spell has been cast. The bird-like figure gestures once
more towards the baby and, looking more closely this
time, you see that the face is more like that of an
animal—a hare perhaps?—with a thin down of fur.
And you can also hear that this small fragile thing is
breathing softly and, with that, see the faint but quick
rising and falling of its tiny chest.*

*

Later that same night Hare also dreams for a second time and, once
again, there is a sense of a sequence or series in play.

94

Hare is looking down at a scene with a figure on a horse who is covered in flowers and with another figure holding the reins. It's spring and the pungent smell of the garlands is overpowering. There's a trumpet or horn call from somewhere and the figure holding the horse's rein gives a tug and begins to walk. As the horse trots along the heavy hidden figure atop sways gently from side to side. Hare looks closer now and on top of this figure there is a small golden crown and the flowers— bluebells, primroses, daffodils—all the Spring clock— have, it seems, been woven into some sort of frame. Hare has the impression of a Spring meadow that has been coiled around this rider, their legs in white stockings and patent leather shoes, visible beneath this living cone. The horse and rider—and figure holding the reins—walk through the village, but the crowds and throngs of people one might expect at a ceremony like this are absent. There is simply a stillness and quietness, except for the clip clopping of the horse's iron clad shoes on the paving stones. Eventually they reach what appears to be a village square where Hare sees that there are now figures. There are eight in all, all dressed in faded rag jackets, with ribbons tied to both elbow and knee. Their faces are painted and the impression— or at least Hare's impression—is that they both belong in this village but are also not from it. Looking again now there are three further figures, dressed the same, but stood away from the others, each with an instrument—a fiddle, a drum, and a hurdy-gurdy with handle. Hare watches as if he is in the crowd that is not there and they begin to play. It's a slow dirge that starts faint with the drone of the hurdy-gurdy, but then increases in volume, the drum joining in, then the fiddle, until it's at quite a pace. The horse backed figure is at the side of all this now, the horse's head bowing and jerking, as the other eight take up their positions opposite one another in a grid like pattern. They raise the sticks they have been carrying—and then clack clack clack, they strike the one of their opposite number, before skipping around and reassembling in the same positions, pausing, then performing the same moves and the clack clack clack again. In between all this Hare can hear the sound of bells that, it is now apparent, are tied to their shoes. And then, as if from nowhere another figure arrives. Running at quite a pace from between two buildings at the side of the square. A figure with ribbons streaming from atop their head. They zig zag this way and that, in and out of the dancers there, then they run around them in circles as if to tie them all up in an invisible knot. And as they do this there's strange sounds coming from that mess of fabric. 'Atschatee! Rabatattatatatee!' It's not an animal exactly. Hare feels that certainly the sounds signify. But Hare cannot understand what this visitor seems to be announcing. And whilst all this commotion is happening, the horseback figure has been led into the centre of the group and the eight dancers are performing some other ritual around them. It involves an angular dance, hands and legs dead straight, then a turning about on one foot towards the figure on the horse. There's a tip of the head as if it's a greeting or mark of respect and as that happens the figure on the horse appears to slightly bow—or, at least, tilt their bulk—to each in turn as if acknowledging some message or offering. The dance is becoming more complex now, different actions and silent communications between the dancers that are also exchanged with the figure atop the horse. At times the music stops and all the figures stop too before the tune starts up once more and all the components begin to *move again. And then, from somewhere not too far off another sound is heard. A different drum and with that striding between two houses another group of six come into the square. Each of them is holding poles on which is either a figure or a head. A fox-like creature and a hare, then one with a painted crown and another with a mass of ribbons trailing down. Other poles have other stranger things atop. The two at the very front are holding poles between which a banner hangs down. It's an embroidered and patchworked landscape of browns and greens. There is a sun and moon in gold and silver cloth—and, above this scene, picked out in different colours that double the ribbons on Ribbonhead's head, the words THE ANCIENT DANCE. The last word is stitched on to the horizon of the hills. And then Hare is flying or hovering up above all of this, looking down as if at a model, the houses, tracks and roads and village square. And there are the dancers in the middle, the procession and garlanded figure on the horse in the centre of it all. It is as if all are painted figures carefully laid out with attention to detail exact. The whole, looking down on it now, is as one of those dioramas that Hare has seen before in a shop or on display. Hare sees a small bronze plaque has been affixed to the base of this scene. Words have been carefully engraved that double those on the banner, but here they are framed and accentuated and with an EVI replacing the AN: THE ANCIENT DEVICE. And now it is as if this scene is a complex object. It is in Hare's hands and is being slowly turned so that all the details and different perspectives can be seen in turn. As if he is himself a giant looking down and through the streets, turning it all carefully beneath a large watchful eye.*

Chapter 15: A Mumming Play

THE ANCIENT DEVICE [*A Mumming Play for Four Parts*].

Parts:
HARE
FOX-OWL
KING JOHN
RIBBONHEAD

[*A theatre-in-the-round demarcated by* HARE, FOX-OWL, KING JOHN *and* RIBBONHEAD *who stand at the edge, each wearing rag jackets*].

ACT I

HARE: [*Enters the round alone, bows low, and speaks*]. What you see here is not what I am. I am not an am nor even an I. Yet this thing—if thing it be—inhabits this other thing I call a body and which here and now answers to the name of Hare. [*He bows again, then steps to one side*].

FOX-OWL: [*Enters and speaks.*] Well said Hare (if that animal is what you are). My turn now to introduce myself and also our play, to set the scene and initiate some action. I Fux-Rowl is no-thing but a fik-shun introducing to you all that are not here a further fik-shun. Four figures on a road and moving—we can only hope—towards a certain place. There to…what? Perhaps—like this here now—perform a play? Certainly, they—that is, we—will present something in language and with gesture. Let's listen in then and hear what they—that is, we—have to say. But first another fik-shun and this one is not a happy sight. [FOX-OWL *steps to one side*].

KING JOHN: [*Enters, stooping slightly, as if carrying some heavy burden on his back*]. It is my onerous duty on this day—as in fact it *always* is—to play a tragic character. A king long deposed, wandering the land and looking for his crown [*he looks up*]. Has anyone seen it? [*All shout things like 'it's over there!' and 'behind you!'*]. I am also looking for my cold throne. In fact, at times I fancy I am already asleep upon it. [*From off-stage someone makes a snoring sound*].

[RIBBONHEAD *has entered the round whilst these introductions are being made. He is silent and sits at the edge of the action, knees bent to his chest, head bowed*].

FOX-OWL: There is something else already here that has yet to speak. [FOX-OWL *looks towards* RIBBONHEAD]. Something which all our discourse can only approximate. Something—let us all at least agree that it is a thing—which we all yearn to meet and, perhaps to host. [FOX-OWL *looks again to* RIBBONHEAD]. Speak thing that is but is also not!

[RIBBONHEAD *remains still and silent*].

KING JOHN: You'll get no joy from that type. He's burnt out. Long gone. The lights are on—possibly [KING JOHN *goes right up to* RIBBONHEAD *bends down and looks closely at the ribbons covering his face, moving his own head up and down and from side to side as if to peer between the ribbons*]—but there's no one home. He is in another place and thirsting for something we cannot here provide. [KING JOHN *looks around and gestures with both his hands*]. Unless anyone happens to have a can? [*All laugh*].

FOX-OWL: Introductions having been made we now come to the main part of our play which is in part a story about another way of doing things that is now gone or has been, let's say, obscured at least [*someone calls out 'What is it then?'*] Well, it's certainly no mystery play that's for sure, but on the other hand no Mummers we know of have performed this particular script. Certainly, things are not now as they

99

were, but here's the rub or we might say, the *pitch* of our
play. Might things return to an earlier state or, more
accurately, is there something in this past that gestures
towards a future? As if our play were intent on locating
points and holes or is itself performing a loop from this
time and place to another [*there are some jeers and groans
from the others*].

KING JOHN: Enough with your prattling Doctor let's get straight
to it. My name is King John and I have been travelling
round and about as part of this caravan here [KING JOHN
gestures broadly to the others], living a life that is less
encumbered by the trappings of the more settled run of
things. Certainly, I have less things to drag me down and
there is less shopping to be done and no bills to be paid
[*someone makes a 'ker-ching' noise as if a cash register has
been opened or closed*]. As long as one avoids the Old Bill
that is [KING JOHN *says this an aside*]. But look, who
comes here! Another fellow and familiar face, though
hidden as always. Someone who is always on the make and,
as it were, has found in this community a snug fit as a hand
is in a glove.

[RIBBONHEAD *gets up and stumbles into the centre of the round
and looks around. He seems somewhat dazed, possibly
drunk*].

RIBBONHEAD: It's true I am always thirsty and looking for a
drink or some such. But then, we're not so different you
and I, both of us—it seems to me—are somewhat lost and
looking for some way to avoid what is. At any rate, I am
further along that road than you but then, perhaps, there is
some wisdom I can offer in exchange for what you might
have in your bag?

KING JOHN: There's nothing for you here fella. Except perhaps the
toe of my boot!

[KING JOHN *leaps towards* RIBBONHEAD *as if to kick him.*
RIBBONHEAD *runs around the round, every so often*
KING JOHN *getting close and kicking—or seeming to kick—*
RIBBONHEAD's *rear*].

100

FOX-OWL: Enough of this comedy! Where's the fourth of us to make this right? Hare, it's your turn now to step up and in.
[HARE *steps somewhat hesitatingly into the round*].
HARE: Well, there's no way I can make all this right, but perhaps I can facilitate some communication between these two or work as mediator?
[RIBBONHEAD and KING JOHN *have stopped running and are looking at* HARE].
HARE: First things first. All of us are in this together and as such are part of the same device. The squabbling and all the rest are also part of the set-up. But it is hoped that by performing it here we will get to a deeper stage of things beneath the fractures and apparent enmities. I think perhaps, for this part, we need a song [HARE *looks at* RIBBONHEAD *who has picked up the hurdy-gurdy and now begins to play*].

ACT II

HARE: Let's act this story out then.
KING JOHN: I'll go first as I usually do in these kinds of set-ups. I was a king upon my road until deposed by this and that and now I'm lost.
RIBBONHEAD: And for my lot? Well, my old lines are that I was brighter once, striding across this landscape without a stoop.
HARE: Time for me to speak my part. Was there perhaps a time when I was not wounded? Certainly, if feels as though this cut [HARE *lifts his shirt and point to his belly*] has always been there.
FOX-OWL: And, finally in this configuration, my part will have been—looking back—to gather you here and put all this out on display so that we might look at it again. To get some perspective on these different aspects. To produce a little wiggle room between and betwixt the different fictions we necessarily partake of.

HARE: Watching you others perform your parts it occurs to me that mine is a part too though less easy is it to shrug off. But let me get deeper in and act it out to see what comes [*with that HARE drops to the ground, curls up in a ball and closes his eyes*]. Here am I now small and fragile, left alone on this moor with none to offer out a hand. My head is full of sadness—and of loneliness too. All that and more I present to you as act.

KING JOHN [*who is now standing at the edge of the round and looking into the middle-distance*]: And for my lot as I've said before I've lost my crown [*which is now lying on the ground next to him*] which signifies to me something precious about who I am and what I used to have. Bereft I am and hurtling towards the end, so it seems, without anyone to accompany me.

RIBBONHEAD [*who is stumbling around the round in an exaggerated manner*]: My part is more apparent even though I necessarily hide my face behind this coloured fabric. I am always looking for something to fill the hole and that thing I take only makes that hole wider and deeper. What have I lost? My compass and desire to get to another place. I'm stuck alright but also blown hither and thither.

FOX-OWL: Well, what a sorry lot and, indeed, what a mess. Each in their own worlds and down the pit. And, although I stand to one side of all of that—and work, as it were, as a proxy audience—nevertheless I have my own issues [*someone shouts out 'hands up who hasn't!'*]. Although directing this lot I also have anxiety about who I am or what it is behind this mask I wear. It seems to me that I am also somewhat lost. Nevertheless, my hunch is that a device like this has its uses if only it can be set up right and, as it were, activated. Let's get it going then and as a start let's switch positions and see what befalls. Perhaps there is another constellation here that will offer some useful information?

[*As if it's a set-up for a dance,* RIBBONHEAD *and* KING JOHN *switch places, as do* FOX-OWL *and* HARE].

FOX-OWL: Now that this has all been further laid out and our other parts taken on let's introduce a further character or not a character as such, more a possibility. A serpent that lies here about.

[*Whilst this is being said* HARE *and* RIBBONHEAD *have covered themselves in a large but shabby piece of gold cloth and from out of the front they hold a pole with a wooden dragon's head. They proceed to circumambulate the round*].

KING JOHN: And so, despite these wounds I already have, it is my lot again to fight this creature that has returned or, perhaps, been summoned by our play if by nothing else.

[KING JOHN *draws a wooden sword and proceeds to strike the Dragon's head. The dragon lunges at* KING JOHN, *there is some clack clack clacking as they move to and fro and fight. At last the dragon gets the better of* KING JOHN *who falls to the ground*].

KING JOHN: I'm got! The dragon's bite is deep, and I bleed. My previous pain is now doubled by this other mark!

[RIBBONHEAD *and* HARE *have now removed the golden cloth and stand there looking down at* KING JOHN. RIBBONHEAD *holds the pole with the dragon's head in one hand as if it's a staff*].

KING JOHN: Is it time now for me to shuffle off or is there someone here—a doctor perhaps?—that can cure what feels to me is perhaps a mortal blow?

[*Whilst this has been going on* FOX-OWL *has taken a small, battered suitcase from the edge of the round and now strides purposefully into the centre of the action*].

FOX-OWL [*now a doctor and gesticulating with his fingers*]: You called for remedy and repair and here I am, ready to heal these wounds with the various wares and other props I have here [*he pulls out a couple of different bottles from his case and in an exaggerated manner dabs and sprinkles them on* KING JOHN *and then shrugs and pours a couple of the bottles down John's throat in an exaggerated manner, peering*

at the bottles to check they have been emptied]. It's no good
your wound is too deep. A more radical cure is needed and
one which will require all of us here to play a part. For that
dragon's bite had poison in it which, now mixed and
mingled with your own royal blood means the end of
you—or at least this fiction you perform.

Chapter 16:

Something Else is Also Here

Ribbonhead gets up and walks into the centre of the round. He stops, stands absolutely still and then in a flurry of ribbons makes a deep bow to the non-existent audience. Once upright again he speaks.

'The time for games and for discourse is over. If you will all now please follow me.'

He then begins to move his legs—slowly at first—in a strange, awkward and angular manner. Each foot is lifted in turn a few inches or so off the ground—though both legs are kept straight— and then placed carefully but purposefully nearby. At the same time, Ribbonhead's arms are outstretched and at a forty-five-degree angle to his body with his fingers pointed downwards parallel to his legs. These moves are then repeated, all of it as if in time to an unheard beat or rhythm. The whole effect is of a compass—or animated sextant perhaps—moving from point to point. After a few more steps, a strange noise comes out of his mouth but also, it seems, from somewhere else altogether.

'Trit-tre-tre-tree! Krit-kre-kre-kree!'

The other three—now standing completely still—are looking on. Not exactly in surprise, but, certainly watchful, alert, as if seeing something that might go off at any moment. Ribbonhead continues, slowly circumnavigating the round with these strange jerky steps.

'Fura-lee fura-lee! Arr-ra-ba-ttee! Arr-ra-ba-ttee!'

The last of these words are shouted out and with that it is as if some larger machine has been activated and the others start to move and then assume their own positions within this diagram that Ribbonhead is drawing out. Ribbonhead's dance—and these odd utterances—are calling to each of them in turn.

Hare is the first to move. His limbs are also straight (which is itself an odd sight) as he sways from point to point, mimicking Ribbonhead. Being smaller—by a head and a half—this has the comic effect of watching some father and son (or, at least, big and little versions of the same). Like Ribbonhead, Hare looks straight ahead, his eyes focused on a point in the middle distance, as he himself begins to travel around the edge of the round.

John, for his part, is slower to begin, as if more reluctant to take up his role in this set-up. Eventually he raises a hand and checks the crown is firmly on his head and walks to the centre of the round and, standing still there, closes his eyes. This has a centrifugal effect on Ribbonhead and Hare, pulling them into an orbit around him. The two of them are both moving more quickly now, like a couple of stretched out canvases or sails. And as these loops are taking place, John (for anyone watching closely) seems to be becoming agitated, or, at least, his breathing is coming and going quicker and quicker. If you listen carefully you can hear the short sharp intakes and gasps out.

At times in this dance—if that's what it is—Ribbonhead gets right up close to John who at these moments—who knows how he knows that this other figure is close?—opens his eyes. Their foreheads nearly touch. When this happens Ribbonhead balances on the balls of one of his feet before falling back on to his other foot (thank goodness he doesn't tumble into John). A threat or an invitation? Is there a question at stake or is it simply an attempt at contact? Exchanges of some kind are certainly being made—John's frown deepens whenever Ribbonhead tilts his own head near—as the diagram is further staked out.

Fox-Owl has also moved to the edge of the round so as to give enough room for all this action to take place. After a few circuits have been made by Ribbonhead and Hare, he takes out a roll of paper from under his jacket—had it always been hidden there? — and coughing once or twice, begins to read aloud.

'Cree-cree can-nee can-nee! Ta-rak-na ter-ree! Skraner-skree! See-rak siree! Nik-nee-sestra-str-stra-strat!'

The speech might well have a comic effect in another setting or in another context (but then the question is *what* context would that be exactly?), but here it is unsettling and out of place. Nevertheless it also makes an odd kind of sense for those who are tuned in—such as the other three here—especially when heard in conjunction with whatever diagram is being drawn by these four together.

'Cre-cree! Saturnalia, neralia, speralia! For youze all this is no longer an invitation! Herappala, harappala, snake-ee ree!'

At times it seems as if Fox-Owl is adlibbing or simply making words up. At others, it is equally clear that he is reading from a script though—could it be?—there seems to be an effort of translation going on before he speaks. The effort is also evident in Fox-Owl's stance. His neck is twisted, shoulders hunched as if trying with all his might to squeeze the words out.

'Te-rappa-pa! Tree-reppa-pa! Cellap-pa! Sera, sera!'

Meanwhile John's face is caught in a grimace of intense concentration. It's as if he is holding on to a line that's caught something big. Something that's far out to sea. He screws his eyes more tightly shut, the frown now completely creasing his face, cheeks quivering, beads of sweat appearing on his forehead.

Ribbonhead and Hare are dancing faster now, Ribbonhead's ribbons flailing about in the cold night air catching the light of their small fire. The whole scene—with these figures moving around inside the ring of stones—is all a flicker. Ribbonhead and Hare have completely synchronised, as if they are, in fact, part of the same fine mechanism, aligning themselves with each other and, indeed, with the landscape around them, but also the sky and stars that, as the performance goes on, are becoming visible above them.

The conjunction of Fox-Owl's speech and this strange dance is almost too much for John to bear, as if the two together is exponentially increasing the force of either one. And John, positioning himself at the centre point is the post around which it all spins. It is as if they are all on some huge carousel that is going faster and faster. Always about to lose control. Always about to go over. But then John is pulling himself—or being pulled perhaps?—back. And the rest of them there are playing their part in sustaining some kind of holding pattern, but one that is always coming close to collapse.

Fox-Owl is still reading as the wind gets up, papers madly flapping in one hand, the other holding his mask on to his head that is bent against the rain that now spits down. Ribbonhead and Hare are completely in synch, moving faster and faster, circumambulating this centre point of John. But Fox-Owl has no awareness of all this—he's not even there—as the words continue to come through him but are certainly not being spoken by him.

*

Later, Fox-Owl takes out the map from that pocket close to his chest and spreads it out flat on the damp moor. It's now the dead of night, but there is a full white moon illuminating the landscape and the circle of stones and group of small figures gathered there.

It is as a dream this scene. Unreal, quiet, watchful.

And there in the centre of the map is that dark spot which, it is now clear, indicates where they have arrived and what now needs to happen at this time and place. Fox-Owl looks briefly up at John who is himself looking down at what's been laid out. Is there a nod or some such communication between the two? At any rate something passes between them and John slowly reaches into his own deep pocket to retrieve that polished silver orb. He carefully places it down on that spot which it is now obvious is a marker for just such a device. And with this gesture something else within that map comes into focus, foregrounds itself from the other sketched out terrain. Another landscape hidden within this one, beneath it somehow and there reflected now in the polished mirror surface.

*

It's a cold and bleak landscape with black hills leading down to a black shore. There are broken pieces scattered along the waterline for all to see, poke, pick up and examine before casting down once more. A black lake of what looks like oil laps up against the black sand. Nearby three burnt and blackened poles have been driven hard into the ground. Atop each one there is a dark shape. A mask or head perhaps? It's too gey to pick out any detail. Up against one of the poles a thin grey figure is slumped, lost and forlorn. Faded and tattered ribbons hide what might once have been a face. And is

108

that a wound in their side and a trickle of dark blood? This figure is bowed and broken. It's clear they have given up and are on the way out. And then looking again and more closely this time there is something else nearby. Curled up by this dreadful scene, in a shallow hollow by the second pole, another creature is lying there that has also seen better days. A small and thin sick hare, eyes bulging, damp body trembling. Then, also standing close by the third pole, a third figure is looking on. Wrapped in a dark cloak, heavy iron crown clamped upon a bowed head. Are they weeping? Certainly, there is a wailing sound that surrounds them. And there is something in their hands. Something it seems that is nearly too heavy to hold.

Fox-Owl speaks quietly. 'It is only on this shore, there amongst the wreckage and broken pieces, that the silver can be found. It is only to those who walk those black hills that something essential is revealed. It is in this place where the other fictions drop away that another kind of meaning can be found. It is down here amongst these darker landmarks that a different kind of story might be written.'

*

That small Hare is in Fox-Owl's arms now. It's the one thing he wants to turn away from but instead he holds it close to his chest. It's definitely ill. Dying perhaps? What would it be to not turn away but instead to turn towards this thing? To hold and cherish this small creature? To carry it even as a totem around his neck? This small animal needs looking after but also, perhaps, can look after him (if he'd let it)? And these other two ghosts. What would it mean to look them both in the eye? And then to hold out his hand to help up that bleeding figure with the hidden face? And to stand unflinching next to that exiled king as he wails? To turn towards these things that up until now he had looked away from? What might the impact be of this turning around on a given script? To let that vast black lake of sadness be always close at hand. To always move in that darker landscape or, at least, to have it as his own place that was always nearby.

Part III

In a Darker Landscape

Chapter 17: Back on the Track

'This walk is like a funeral procession' says John as they march in single file along the trackway. It's true that there is a silence surrounding them and a new and sombre quality to their journey as if they have passed over some threshold and are indeed walking towards some final destination, where, perhaps, they are to put something to rest.

'Yes, it all has the feeling to me that this is not just a pilgrimage in the land of the living but as if we are also wandering in—or perhaps through—another landscape' says Hare. 'Of the Dead.'

There is a pause as there they go along one after the other.

'Well', says Fox-Owl, 'this would be entirely in keeping with our play which, after all, is partly about that other land—or, at least, a landscape that is darker than the more usual one.'

There is another pause and then John speaks again as he trudges along. 'I'm not sure I signed up for this kind of journey. I've enough problems in the land of the living to want to go wandering about in the land of the dead.' Another pause. 'There's certainly a few there that I don't want to meet, that's for sure.'

Ribbonhead, who had been quiet up to that point, speaks up from the back. 'Well, if it's the land of the dead we're walking through then there are a few ghosts here that owe me a thing or two so perhaps that can be sorted out as we go.'

As they've walked and talked a little more, the surrounding landscape has indeed got darker. A mist has got up too and is curling around their ankles. Occasionally there are wisps also that obscure the view. As they trudge along, clouds also pass over what seems now as if it is a full moon there hanging in the sky like a silver orb. The clumps of trees, mounds and other features to either side of them are silver and grey, set against a deep and dark blue background. It certainly feels as if they are walking through a different kind of landscape. Nothing stirs and there are no noises—where are the birds?—except their feet crunching on the chalk path and the occasional brush of a branch from an overgrown hedge against their clothes.

It occurs to John as he marches along that trackway that the drum he carries is the thing that must be put to rest (it certainly can't be played, at least not by him). He can feel it getting heavier in his pack. In fact, reflects John as he walks along, it feels as if it's from this other landscape they are now passing through. It doesn't belong in the landscape of the living, he's sure about that. At any rate it needs to be put down somewhere as it's increasingly an unwelcome burden on his back.

Ribbonhead speaks up again from the back. 'John, can I give you hand with your pack? It looks to me as if it's weighing you down. A burden shared is a burdened halved. Why not pass it here a while?'

John grunts and hitches the bag up higher on his back. 'It's easy enough for me to carry, I certainly don't need no help from you.'

'You say that John, but we're here in the land of the dead.' Ribbonhead gestures with his hands to the increasing darkness and the brooding shadows on either side of them. 'In this place it's easy to get weighed down with this and that and stumble and then, what? You wouldn't want to fall and twist an ankle in this place.'

Hare lets out a nervous laugh as John just grunts and increases the speed of his walk.

*

At one point they come across a sea marsh—they must be near the coast. There is salt in the air and soft and spongy ground into which their feet sink. But just as the brackish water begins to reach their ankles a raised plank is there, placed across a series of other sticks thrust into the marsh and criss-crossed so as to make a platform. They carefully step on to this rough construction one by one. The wood is old and black from the salt water. It's also slippery in places but, thank goodness, held fast by the stakes driven deep into the ground. Along it goes more or less straight across this marsh, leading them further into the mist.

One by one, one foot after the other, they carefully traverse this new trackway.

Looking down from the planks into the pools at either side, they can see there are things in the water there half submerged, as if discarded. More props perhaps? Most seem broken or certainly redundant. But then elsewhere alongside those dark planks it is as if other objects have been placed deliberately, left for others to pick up and use in turn or perhaps for some other purpose or, indeed, for some other agency. Some of these look tempting. After all, we all need some props to help us make it through. But it's also clear that in this place things really need to be left behind rather than accrued.

Along they step, careful not to put a foot wrong (although what would a wrong step be in a place like this?). The atmosphere is one of palpable anxiety. It's in them but also in the very landscape itself, as if each is mirroring the other. It seems as if an overwhelming 'what if' is in play within that marsh and that they cannot but progress ever further towards the middle and towards the very thing they fear.

Fox-Owl speaks up from the front. 'This is the dangerous time when all can easily be lost. Look to how you place your feet and do not look to either side, especially if you see anything glinting or moving or that otherwise appears to grab your attention.'

But the warning comes too late. Ribbonhead is already down on two knees staring into a silvery pond. He is entranced or at least affixed by whatever it is he sees there. And John too is suddenly dropping down on one knee gesturing out his right arm as if to hold another's hand there or help someone out.

Hare shouts out. 'It's all mists and illusion! Both of you come to your senses! There is nothing here for you or for any of us!'

Fox-Owl has turned and retraced his steps. He is at John's side now and gently puts his hands on John's shoulders. John's head bows a little further down, there is a sigh and with that he brings back his arm from that edge, closes up the open hand into a fist, and gets slowly to his feet. Hare is at Ribbonhead's side also. He does not touch him but simply stands and looks at what has captured Ribbonhead's gaze. The pool is smooth and like a mirror and in it is the double of that Ribbonhead kneeling there on the plank, although the ribbons are darker in the reflection, or somewhat obscured by the mist. Fox-Owl has come over now and also looks down. He then reaches over and gently clasps Ribbonhead by the shoulders.

'Yes, that's an image of you alright, but don't be deceived. It is only an image and not to be believed. You see only what you want to see here, when this means also what you fear. This image is what you are now and indeed will leave behind. It is not for what you will become or for where you move towards.'

He gently lifts Ribbonhead to his feet. The ribbons are damp and lank as they brush against Fox-Owl's hand. Ribbonhead's body, to Fox-Owl, feels thin and brittle. Far out in the mist they hear the call of some marsh bird as if in acknowledgement of the trial they have just been through or, perhaps, to signal its end. It's cold and the marsh mist is now reaching up to their knees.

And then they're off again along the planks, careful this time to keep their eyes focussed on the next step ahead and not the ditches and pools to either side.

*

Eventually a final black plank takes then to firmer ground. They have reached an island of sorts within the marsh. Or, at least, they have arrived at a slightly raised ground within this glittering maze of waterways and pools. Walking to the centre of this place they find a pole stuck into the ground. It's thick, the size of a felled mature tree, shaped and smoothed by careful hands, but with long grooves left as perhaps they were rather than carved in. Looking up they cannot see the top—it's shrouded in that mist—but looking more closely at the pole there are further black marks or patches, dried out tar or some such substance that has, perhaps, dripped down from way up above. They have it seems arrived at some other dark centre here. It's a place they have themselves been circling, although its equally clear that the raised wooden platform has led them directly here. It's still and cold and as they look again at the post it seems as if the black tar—if that's what it is—is still slowly coming down the grooves of that dark wood.

It's getting darker now and Ribbonhead has sat down, his back leaning against that cold hard pole. John is looking up into the mist to see if he might glimpse what is atop—the mist has cleared a little—whilst Hare is busying himself thinking about where they might camp or make a fire or at least take some rest. But all this business of Hare's is of no avail. There's nothing here to do or see— and nowhere comfortable for them to rest. Nowhere that is away from this dark pole. Fox-Owl is also standing still within the gloom and, at last remarks, 'This is another centre we circle about. It's waiting for us always in our dreams but also on this marsh island here. It's the business of our travels to avoid places like this even though, clearly, they attract us in some senses and this one has reeled us in.'

He pauses and looks up to the top of the pole. 'Here all things are weighed up and found wanting.' He turns and looks back along the way they have come. 'It's maybe why so much has been discarded on the way.' His voice is quieter than usual, more reflective or as if he is talking to himself. 'Is it still a performance then? Certainly, it's another representation that has been made to figure something that cannot be said or hitherto shown. It is that making of something dark in this place that shows to us and any other traveller who makes it here that all this will always end and that the ending always arrives too soon and comes as a shock.' He looks back up the pole. 'It's a reminder to us all.'

*

It's not an easy night for any of them. It's cold and wet and none of them gets much sleep. And then, when they do stir, Ribbonhead is nowhere to be seen. It's not that unusual. He's often left at dawn to find something if he can. Hare is busy looking through bags and pockets for any food or anything else that might help get them started. John grunts and turns over in his bag. Fox-Owl is the only one up and alert. Breath like smoke in the cold morning air, he's looking up at the pole as the sun begins to show on the horizon.

'Look' he says, 'the mists have all cleared and you can nearly see the top.'

Hare pauses and looks up. The sky is now pink and orange. The birds have begun their morning calls and it seems indeed as if the top of the pole is indeed visible. It must be over a hundred feet high and there is something shining affixed to the top. It's difficult to make out exactly what it is or what it's made of. In this light, it looks to be of gold. It seems to be an object of sorts. It could be a face or certainly some kind of creaturely representation. But it might also be something more plant-like or simply a stone. Looking up, one can just about make out some details. Scratches or engravings perhaps. At any rate, it's certainly something unexpected. There it is shining at the top as the sun rises and more of the pole is lit up orange.

The sky is taking on a brighter blue now and there are birds also circling the top of the pole.

Hare is looking up towards the top and nods with his head as he speaks as if to the pole itself. 'I recognise something about that thing up there—or a detail of it, if that makes sense—from a dream perhaps or some other fiction, I'm not sure.'

'Yes, it doesn't seem to really belong here' says Fox-Owl who is also looking up. 'It's almost as if', there is a pause, 'someone has come to this place in the dead of night while we slept, and replaced whatever it was that *was* up there with this new thing.'

John has stirred and props himself up. He looks at Hare and Fox-Owl then up to the top of the pole. He frowns and squints. 'It seems to me that it's a head with a crown up there. I fancy a closer look.' He gets up briskly and examines the pole around which they have set up their camp. It's smooth to the touch, although there are the same grooves they saw last night and some ridges and the odd bump, but certainly nothing for him to get his hands on. The black liquid is also not there. John turns to Hare. 'What do you think Hare? Can you climb this pole and get a better look?'

Hare looks up then down again. Then silently he moves towards the pole, reaches out both of his arms and begins to climb, legs curled tight around the pole, one arm after the other, pulling up and squeezing tight. What a sight this is, a performance alright, here in the middle of this marsh with no one there but them to see.

Ribbonhead is back. His feet and legs are soaking wet and he's breathing heavy. 'What's happening here then? Has Hare become a steeplejack amongst everything else?'

John speaks. 'So, you're back then. Did you find anything you're after? No, I didn't think so. Face it. There's nothing hidden in this marsh—except, perhaps, this thing.' He gestures with a nod to the top of the pole and to Hare, now a smaller figure as he climbs higher and higher.

Fox-Owl calls out. 'Careful Hare. If you slip, you'll burn your hands! And make sure you save enough energy for the descent!'

But this is lost on Hare who can hardly hear what's being said or shouted up. He's two thirds up the pole already and himself nearly out of breath. He can't look up or down or he'd lose his grip, so it's one hand after the other as he keeps up going bit by bit.

And then he's arrived at the top. This thing above brushes his head. Hare steels himself and looks up. For some reason it's difficult to focus and see exactly what this thing is despite being so close. It's certainly golden in colour, but that might also be the sun that has lit it right up. There are also further details demarcating what seems a face, large eyes, a nose and mouth, and then there are further lines and marks around these features. It's looking at him, smiling there. But then it's not that at all but something else altogether. A landscape picked out in three dimensions, wrapping itself around this pole. There are hills and valleys, tracks and grids, all in gold as if this thing has been crafted by some tremendously skilled smith. Then looking again, it's now none of this at all but simply a smooth inverted cone-like shape, the apex affixed to the top of the pole. Looking closer now and it's as if the cone is spinning at an incredible speed. And even as if there are golden flecks or sparks coming off it as it turns and turns. And then looking further and into the spinning gyre it's as if there are other details there within the details. Flat planes with further landscapes and then with other passages between. Hare is now looking right into the golden fire and in there he suddenly sees as clear as crystal and in a still part at the very centre of it all, a scene all laid out. A pole with something affixed atop. And around that pole three figures looking up—his companions all marked out in exact detail as if painstakingly made, painted and placed there. And yes, on that other pole within this scene there it is, another figure clasping tight. A second Hare looking up at this thing that is on top. And this other thing, small and detailed, golden in the dawn light is as an exact replica of that which Hare is looking at and lost in now.

Fox-Owl calls up from below. 'What is it Hare? Can you report back?'

There's no response from Hare, but as they watch this tiny figure begins the descent, hand over hand, legs once again squeezed tight. It's Hare who's coming down alright, but he's somehow golden in this light. Indeed, the sun is picking out the detail of Hare's head and body which makes it seem as if Hare himself is a moveable part of this device set up here. As if the latter is now lowering down part of its mechanism as part of its workings out.

Hare reaches the ground. He catches his breath, rubs his hands together and looks at them all. 'I can't say exactly what it is up there, but I can say this. There are more parts to this ancient device than we were first aware.' He pauses then continues. 'And our performance seems to have set things in motion that it seems to me are beginning to have far reaching consequences in other places besides this one.'

Chapter 18: The Jetty and the Ship

After a meagre breakfast they pack their few things and retrace their steps along the planks. This time they are more careful to keep their eyes straight ahead and to make sure each foot is firmly on that plank. Finally, they step back off the last plank onto solid ground and can see that the main track actually goes around the marsh. Fox-Owl seems especially surprised that this way was not clear to them the night before. He looks along that path and then back the way they came, tilts his head slightly then shakes it. All of them pause for a moment or two and then off they go on this other track.

The path goes through scrub and grass, up towards a ridge which they then traverse in single file. A little further on and they reach the coast.

Coming down from that ridge towards the beach they can also see what seems to be a jetty of sorts, set like a black tick against the blue grey of the sea. It looks as if it's been abandoned some time ago. Walking along the shoreline now there are old and broken concrete posts and bits of rusty metal in amongst the rocks and driftwood. It's slow work with more than one slip and stubbed toe. At the jetty now and they can see that the concrete is also cracked and stained and that some of the steps that lead down to the water are broken. But there is also evidence of some kind of relatively recent industry here. There are large oil barrels tucked in near to the steps leading up to the jetty top and some chalk marks demarcating figures perhaps and, possibly, words in capitals albeit faint and unclear. These have been sketched on that wall at points along the jetty path where the different sets of steps go down to the water. The sea is rough and churning, occasional spits and sprays are thrown up to the jetty path making the whole set-up—it seems to our travellers—treacherous.

It's not clear what kind of ship would dock at a jetty like this here in this dark landscape—or what its cargo would be. Certainly, looking more closely at the barrels now they are very old, most are empty although one or two still feel partly full. Behind the barrels they also find a makeshift camp of sorts. Or, at least, there is a tarpaulin that has been pulled tight and secured on some rusty hooks set in the jetty wall. Beneath this, there are a couple of pallets and some old pieces of carpet and bits of cloth. It's relatively dry at least and, looking closely, it seems as if perhaps a few others had slept here recently as there are also some ragged blankets scattered about. There is also evidence of a little shrine of sorts. Or, at least there is a platform made from pallets with planks across and on top of that a couple of candle stubs and a few other bits and pieces that look to have been scavenged from the beach. A large old rusty nail. A weather-beaten piece of driftwood in the shape of an animal or at least something with eyes and legs. A stone with a hole that has been threaded with an old salt encrusted thin piece of rope. The weather is closing in now and they feel spits of rain through the gaps between tarpaulin and wall as well as the occasional spray from the sea.

Fox-Owl gestures with his fingers to indicate the steps up the jetty side, and then, one by one, they take the steep stairs—which are indeed slippery—up to the jetty top. Up here the wind is howling and blows their increasingly damp clothes close against their skin. Fox-Owl, head bent against the wind, one hand holding the mask on tight, begins the walk along. There are no walls or rails, and the jetty top is itself slightly sloped from one side to the other. A slip here might well mean a tumble into the sea—and there are certainly no lines or rings to be thrown into the black. Anyone going in now would certainly be lost to the depths.

It's slow progress, but eventually the four of them reach the jetty's end. It's a steep black shelf and drop down towards the deep and wild and black sea. Occasionally they fancy they can see a further platform or shelf down there, blacker than the jetty they are on. The moon is out now and every so often gazes down from a gap in the clouds that race across the sky.

Fox-Owl is looking outwards now towards the horizon and then suddenly raises the hand not holding the mask and points toward something out there. A smudge of sorts on the horizon line. A ship perhaps? The smudge gets larger as they watch for a few minutes. Although it's not clear there are any sails or masts, it is more simply an irregular black shape against the black. As they watch for a few minutes more it moves closer and closer until some detail can be seen. It's a huge black barge with a cabin and other structures on the deck. There is indeed no mast, although there are thinner poles and lines that suggest some kind of sailing apparatus.

Closer still now.

A grey wall with deep scratches and scrapes and other markings. It moves smoothly through that rough sea as if guided by a giant hand or held down by a heavy ballast. And there, on the side of the hull, picked out in in a lighter grey, scratched and obscure, but readable, a name.

THE GARE.

The ship comes closer to the platform they are standing on and they can see the deck is strewn with various objects. They are all rusted or at least painted tar black. Is that an old engine? And a small crane perhaps? Then other bits and pieces that are less easy to identify. And there is the cabin there although they can see no figure within or indeed on deck.

And then, suddenly and surprisingly, there is a flash of light. Then another. It's coming from the top of one of the poles affixed to the hull. A pause and then another longer flash shines out. More follow thick and fast. A sequence of short and longer flashes. It seems as if something is being communicated to them on the shore—or at least, an attempt is being made to reach across that gulf.

They watch as the ship moves in front of the jetty like a sliding piece of land. It feels unreal to have this cliff moving in the sea. And then the ship has passed and is drifting or sailing further off. Its huge bulk cleaving a path through the rough sea. A few minutes more and it's a black mark on the horizon again and going further out.

Fox-Owl turns, head bent against the wind and begins the slow walk back, the others following. The wind begins to die down slightly as they walk. Ribbonhead stumbles more than once and has to be held fast by a grunting John. They reach the stairs down from the jetty top and from there they make their way towards the barrels and the camp behind. They're damp and cold and there's little there to warm them up except for the ragged blankets. But Hare breaks out a little dry food and lights the candle stubs, which they now sit huddled around. No one has spoken for perhaps the last hour, but it's there with them in the glow of the candlelight. That ancient dark hull that came close and sent something across.

*

That night the ship moves in and out of dreams and sleep. Its bulk pressing in. Its one light flashing on and off. And sometimes one or another of them wakes and pulls the tarp fast or checks the others sleeping there, perhaps pulling a blanket over feet or shoulders. And then at one point in the very dead of night Fox-Owl is not there. He has gone back alone along the jetty top and to that dark shelf. There he is, a dark figure right at the jetty's end. Wrapped in a ragged blanket for a coat, one hand holding the mask fast. He's looking out for that ship, waiting to see if it has more messages for them. Perhaps even that it might dock? And would he then step on? Leave this shore and the others sleeping here? It's not clear even to Fox-Owl himself. Would he be able to get back if he left on that ancient ship? It seems to him that it might well be a one-way trip. But then a further thought follows quick and close and haunts him for some time after. What, exactly, is there to get back for?

Chapter 19: Down into the Basement

The night turns imperceptibly into day.

The same dark skies and the same lashing rain are there when Hare peeps out from beneath the tarp. They're all damp and tired after a restless night. All except Ribbonhead that is, who has once again disappeared out into the first dawn light. Hare lights what's left of the candles and rustles arounds once again in bags and pockets. There isn't really anything left to eat. They'd relied on buying some food on the way or, at a pinch, catching a fish. Fox-Owl is up and, after looking pointedly at Hare and John, he makes a suggestion.

'It's not a day for walking this, but perhaps we might take this opportunity of everything being overcast to rehearse a little more?' He looks around the camp. 'In fact, I'd say this place here is not a bad round to act some things out, or, perhaps, get a little deeper into our parts and see what they are about.'

As he says this last sentence Fox-Owl begins circumambulating the camp, running his hand over the rough jetty wall and peering at some more of the chalk marks there, checking the tarp is still tight and then also clearing some space in the middle. He moves the pallets and mats, and then also what might have been that small shrine. And then with a piece of chalk he conveniently finds he demarcates a large circle in front of them.

'Here we go then.' He points with the chalk to the circle drawn there. 'A space set aside from the everyday, but also at the very centre of things.'

'I'm not sure that's going to work as a stage.' John nods at the circle. 'I'm also not keen on looking out all our props.' He frowns. 'If it's all the same to you I think I'll sit this one out.'

'Come on John, this is a rare opportunity. Here we all are and now here is also a circle to step up and into. Perhaps to tell a story?

My idea here is that we can further explore the narratives that brought our characters here—or, perhaps even invent some further back stories.' He looks at the other two in turn. 'You know, to flesh things out a little more.'

'I'm not very good at making things up', says Hare as he looks at the chalk marks with a bit of a frown. 'Although it's also true that I've always got a few narratives running around my head so perhaps that might work.' He bites his lip and makes a little nod.

'Exactly', says Fox-Owl. 'All you need do is step up and over the mark and see what comes. Treat it as a bit of a challenge.'

There's a groan from John who has sunk down deeper into his bag. At the same time there is a sudden gust of cold air as the tarpaulin is lifted up from the outside and a sodden Ribbonhead is there peering in. He pauses, one hand holding up the tarp, looking at the others and the circle there.

'Have I missed something or is it that something is about to start?'

'You ain't missed nothing' says John. 'In point of fact, you're back just as it's your turn.' He nods his head towards Fox-Owl. 'Our director here has a little plan for this rainy day and it involves you stepping up—for a change—and into that demarcated space there', he nods to the circle, 'and inventing a fiction or laying out more of the fiction you already are. I wasn't quite clear which was meant.'

'Precisely' says Fox-Owl. 'It is as John says. We have an opportunity here to do a little more work around these roles we play and, well, to get deeper underneath some of that material. Perhaps even identify some sequences that have been hitherto obscure.'

Fox-Owl gestures with both arms to the whole area underneath the tarp and within a gloom that is lit only by the few spluttering candles.

'Imagine if you can that this is a basement of sorts and that we have all now slipped down into it.'

There is a quietness, even the rain has stopped.

The candles flicker.

All of them are looking into that centre and deeper into that gloom now.

Fox-Owl continues, his voice is quieter and more serious. 'Things are different down here than they are in the world above. Down here the usual coordination points—all those different stories that everyone holds so dear—no longer hold. You come here empty handed. It's the only way to make it through. And the images that appear in this place—are they summoned, or do they come of their own accord?—are more present.'

He looks at each of his companions in turn.

'They need to be taken very seriously indeed.'

Hare speaks up. 'I'm not sure I like it down here.'

Fox-Owl again. 'It's a place that no one wants to go that's for sure, although here's the thing. Some intention is always working away against that reluctance. Undoing all those carefully laid plans about this and that.'

Ribbonhead has come further in now and is dripping on the concrete floor. 'It feels familiar to me somehow this dark place, as if I've been here before.' Ribbonhead points at the candles and mats and pallets. 'Or at least I seem to recognise something about the details and other props that are here.'

John frowns as Ribbonhead speaks.

'Well', says Fox-Owl, 'it just needs one of us here willing to say something along the lines of 'this is me!' and then not simply to say it, but also to *show* it. Then if that gesture is sincere, or, at least, seen and heard as such, the work can begin.' He looks pointedly at each of them in turn. 'It's different for everyone, but in many ways always the same. Everyone knows that there is this dark basement there beneath their feet, just waiting for such a visit.'

'Christ', says John, 'that's some speech, even for you. It's quite something you're asking of us here.'

Hare turns his head to the side and strokes the back of his neck. Ribbonhead looks as though he's making ready to leave again—or perhaps he is in fact making ready to step up and in?

Fox-Owl looks around them all once more.

'It's always a risk, that's for sure. To step up and into the middle and say something real. Something along the lines of 'this is how it is!' To *really* say that rather than beating around the bush. The risk, when all is said and done, is that a judgement will be made and rejection will follow. It's the biggest of risks because it's the smallest of things that has stepped out. But, on the other side of all that anxiety there are rewards to be won. Although that can never really be known until one steps up and over the line. That kind of knowledge—if knowledge it is—is only for those looking back over their shoulder. Seeing the darker landscape suddenly lit up as if by a sun that is momentarily uncovered by the clouds.'

Fox-Owl pauses then looks around the gloom.

'Who wants to go first?'

Chapter 20: All of Them are Wounded

Awkward and a little hesitant, Ribbonhead gets up and steps into the middle to see what comes. From one point of view this is a wretched and ragged figure, passing by and passed by. Shirt untucked and stained. There is something broken here and always on the verge of coming apart. But from another point of view this is also a very real thing. Wounded perhaps—like all of them there—but not quite out for the count. Ribbonhead shouts out clearly and loud as a bell.

'Look! I am here!'

And, indeed, there he is standing in the middle of them all, as if a bolt of lightning had suddenly struck.

It's quiet except for the rain on the tarpaulin and after a pause he begins his tale. It's a story of wandering around and about and looking away from what he has now made the decision to turn and face. There's no rescuing this figure and no one watching on steps in to salve any of the wounds on display.

Ribbonhead knows it is to himself that he especially tells his tale. There is no-one else there to be what he needs (although perhaps one or two of the others might be called on to act out a part) and there is no rewriting the history books. Part of what this particular performance is all about is putting things in place so that Ribbonhead can split, become both the one who needs and the one who gives. To be who he is right here and now and then, also, who he might become by looking on and finally grasping the particular set-up that is now on display. The doubling is the method.

An acting out and a watching that act.

Such a simple device, but also the most difficult of all. To be the hand reaching out for help and the hand that helps you up.

In this darker landscape the hills are black, the woods dense and damp. Brambles and briars scratch the skin. Down here there are very few places to stop and rest. This is a forsaken place. But it is also here that Ribbonhead feels most alive. Alongside the darkness and the driving rain, a thin thread of joy is woven in. It's real and so am I. And, with that, a further feeling—could it be?—of strength and power that this is, at last, being faced. That all that stuff that had kept him away was just a story he had told himself to keep him from coming down.

And with this the whole set-up tips once more and something else begins to foreground itself. Dappled sunlight reaches those dark and damp groves. Clean, dry air to breath as if on a high hilltop. It's here that Ribbonhead finds the thing he's been after. Cool, clean water to drink from a brook and something else. Something precious, glinting just beneath the surface of that water. A jewel or prism—rays of different colours, reds, blues, greens and golds—right there, his for the taking. Something very nearly in reach which when seen—and grasped—will allow yet another kind of focus.

How many other Ribbonheads with their faces hidden have made this journey before? How many more will step into that round or somewhere similar and walk this darker landscape once more? Each begets the next. And each attempts to break the cycle. To stand up and turn around. And with that, at last to take responsibility for the decisions they have made and what they have become and, more importantly, for what might then occur.

It is as if this darker landscape were itself an agency that has simply used Ribbonhead as its own platform so as to make it through—waiting for a pause, some hesitation in all the business as usual. Ribbonhead is the conduit through which this now flows. His own memories at first. Images of the places he has been and things he has seen on the road. Then other memories from much further back and further afield come thick and fast. Other figures, then animals, plants. The rivers and stones. Here all the world comes rushing, eager to pass through this temporary gap. Ribbonhead sees—and *feels*—all of this. An endless round of small realisations and revelations, of identifications and soundings. He is both the vessel and the passageway. Ribbonhead smiles beneath those ribbons, then laughs out loud: 'I am the gap through which the world pours!'

It needs this fragility, this wounded creature, so as to perform its task. It has no time—no time at all—for those that walk too straight a line. With them there is no way in or out. All is sealed up to make what is separate and which then walks around as its own proud thing. For there must be something more porous, or, at least, with chinks. It's the suffering which lets something else come through. It's the ruptures and holes—experienced as wounds and cuts from this side—that allow this travel from one place to the next. Allow also the world to come in and be felt.

And in all of this Ribbonhead himself is nearly all used up. Burnt out like the proverbial flame that burns so bright. What he was has become an instrument for this other thing and its purpose. In fact, something of his self is still there, but it's no longer small. Or, at least, this smallness is the tiny cut that has allowed this other circuit to run and run and with that, this other vast thing to come pouring through.

*

Way back when, before he was even Hare, he had entered into a bargain. It hadn't been explicit, but both parties had known—on some level—that an arrangement had been set up and, with that, that there had been some kind of contract made. Indeed, back then it had not felt like any bargain, but more simply a sharing. Suddenly there were two of them together drawing out a shared diagram. Hand in hand, running across a meadow in the rain. Scripts being swiftly re-written. Commitments wordlessly made.

Little did either know that something else was stirring here. Something that had its own momentum and, as such, a very specific future trajectory that would pull them in its wake. Something was already up ahead. Waiting for them.

When push came to shove both felt hurt and, especially for Hare, betrayed. 'But we had a bargain!' He would mumble endlessly to himself, trying to understand how such a thing could be broken and what it meant, now, to have been betrayed. In his darkest hours he would reflect that his life up to that point had been a dense forest of bargains with this just being the latest. Some still held, but others—deeper bargains—had been broken long ago. Even, he sometimes thought, before he had been born. In fact, his intuition—often in the dead of night—was that he had been born *into* a broken bargain or was somehow the result of a broken bargain that he now had to carry as if it were a heavy stone. Something, certainly, was there somewhere deep down that needed to be fixed. There was, he thought, a set-up behind this particular set-up, and, behind that, yet another. A sequence or nesting of these broken bargains, each begetting the next, each setting up a further fiction to obscure whatever it was that had come before.

It was all this that had set him running, as if by this method he might escape the consequences of his latest betrayal (whatever that happened to be). But, of course, all this followed him. There it was, waiting for him wherever he ended up. A silent companion standing at his shoulder, watching silently on as he attempted to make his way around and about.

But was there something else in play here too? Something besides the betrayal?

There would be rare moments—who knows exactly how or why—when he would quite suddenly stop, turnabout, and then look directly at all this as if it had been laid out for him to examine. At these times he would come face to face with whatever was behind the betrayal and, indeed, of all the betrayals reaching right back. And always, at these times, there would be a sharp pang of loss. And then, with that, a sense of nearly overwhelming grief. In this loneliest of places, if he could bare to stay and look, he would sometimes see another path marked out, barely trodden, but, yes, looking closely, definitely there. A faint imprint on the damp grass.

What would it mean to let go of this bargain—broken as it was—was that even possible? Certainly, not as he was. It was the bargain that gave him a sense of self. And a broken bargain, although painful, worked in much the same way. Indeed, what would he be without this burden that he carried? Is 'he' anything but this he would wonder?

But at those rare times there it was plain to see. A different way ahead was apparent. Grief, if it could be borne, held something else besides the sadness. Or even, thought Hare, there was a more secret knowledge *within* the sadness.

It was this memory that he also carried with him. Something nearly not there to pitch against the loss. And when, at last, he found himself, on that faint path again (who knows who or what had shown the way?) it was always loss—his sense of losing something precious—that operated as the compass. It was at these times that he understood that it was never going to be the case that he would find this thing he once had had (if, indeed, that had ever been the case). It had long gone. Or, rather, that being on this path and with his loss was the thing itself. The trick, so he discovered, was to take all of this and claim it as his own. To fold the sadness inside. To place it, as it were, inside a box. To keep it safe and secret in a place that was his alone.

It was then that this thing called Hare was born. He felt like a hare so why not? Perhaps he was one? And it would be this Hare who would maintain a fidelity to his wound. It could be seen in his stoop and occasional stammer and nervous glances around. He would embody it. Carry it with him. Follow its lead.

Had there been other Hares before him (and would there be others to come)? Had a fiction like this also been lived out by those others? Was it even perhaps a fiction that was written in the genetic code? Certainly, Hare felt that his blood had itself been betrayed or compromised somehow. His very look—creased brow, lines around mouth and the deep sockets of his eyes—all of it evidenced, it seemed to Hare, some deeper destiny at work beneath his own consciousness.

Something had been written in flesh and bone, that he was now living out.

And so as well as any other road he happens to be on, Hare also follows this other faint path. Its way stations look less like the stages of a worked out path and more like cairns on hill tops haunted by ghosts. But there it was nevertheless. A faint spiral path that climbed slowly out of the endless circuits he had previously followed. Hare's betrayal from the perspective of this other path was in fact something else. Something had needed to be broken so that this other perspective could at last be set up.

*

Once John had been married. At first the world had opened up as they had shared experiences, excavated histories and projected dreams. Small tokens had been exchanged, risks taken and reciprocated. To no longer be alone, what a feeling! For John it was to have someone there who loved him. To be looked after. Ultimately it was to be affirmed as who he was. And for him, it was, at last, to have something else to look after too. In such a state all wounds temporarily heal. All things are quicker and lighter. Even the winter and the darkness come calling as friends.

Not that there hadn't been frictions and flash points, moments when rough edges met. Disagreements certainly occurred, but these were all subsumed within the larger project of two together.

But then came the day, that then became days, when the occasional frictions were more prolonged, sharp and damaging, and then—so it seemed all at once—there was less passion to salve those fresh wounds (or had the old ones simply been re-opened?). Arguments that had once been a point of interest became difficult. Resolutions hard to find. No punches were thrown, but crockery was. Each would then retreat, alone, to lick their wounds.

Or, at least, this was John's take on things. Who knows how much of it relates to what actually went on? There are always two sides. Two points of view (at least). Perhaps he was an abuser of sorts? Certainly, there were signs that might be interpreted as such and even John himself would sometimes doubt his version of things. Eventually she had turned to him and said, simply and quietly (as if already speaking from a far-off place).

'I've got to go now.'

And left.

A story then with an ending that was predictable enough. But what if this familiar narrative could have been turned around somehow? Perhaps there could have been a way through all this. Not a return to that blessed state, but a seeing of the present set-up as a kind of work. Was there perhaps some knowledge to be gained here?

All the fights came down to this. A sense of hopes and dreams dashed on the rocks. Each of them had then closed up, tightened their grasp around a small precious thing.

So, what was in John's tight fist if he could have uncurled those fingers to take a look? Certainly, there would have been an image of the two of them together, carefree and happy. Everything to come. What else? A future home and children perhaps. What else? Other adventures and travels together certainly. What else? In a truck or caravan, travelling towards some stones. A part of something. A band or group perhaps? And then, beneath this, deeper still in that tight fist, an image of John himself perhaps by a riverbank or at the edge of a wood. Standing there and stripped to the waist, laughing. Dancing. Something rushing through him.

And with all that a feeling that the world was, once again, at his feet.

All of these images formed a constellation that was John's and so, if something had been messed up somewhere along the line, then it was his own business so to speak. As if, in fact, she had simply stumbled into—and then been broken by—a story that was not hers (and then there was also the fact that he had no doubt betrayed her story too). Perhaps it is only in relation to one another that these darker landscapes and narratives are finally seen?

John remembers, on his birthday many years ago, a close friend handing him a gift, and shouting out clearly and loud as a bell.

'Freedom!'

John had uncurled his fist then alright and looked down at this small hard object that had been passed his way. A large iron nail, bent in the middle.

Most of these images were familiar to John. They had all come out before. They were images that reinforced a sense of his self that had always been in place. But were there other images also somewhere 'in' there, less familiar, less human even. Images that were behind these different versions of John. What might they be about?

What if the self were not a thing to be fathomed or, indeed, discovered, but, rather, was there to be un-made then re-made?

Constructed anew? What if all these memories and narratives had first to be cleared out so as to allow that other work to begin? Here perhaps was the freedom John desired (or, at least, something within him desired). Not to return to or rediscover a self. Not to finally understand who he 'really' was. But more radically perhaps to make himself anew. To see what himself as something else might be. To write his own fiction. To be the king of his own kingdom.

A curled fist then yes, but also a project. To attempt to reconfigure his take on these images and figures that came out of that closed fist. To see them not as 'his', but as images and figures that passed through a landscape. Not then to endlessly turn them around a particular self-definition (and sense of loss)—as if he were the only centre of some map—but to follow these images and figures elsewhere and to embrace any surprises they might bring. It was this that John longed for. Simply a bit of flexibility. To be able to identify with more than the limited set-up he had, so it seemed, been given. It was this, perhaps, that the bent nail really meant. Not only a turn away from what was already laid out but also a repurposing of what lay at hand for a who knows what that was yet to come.

*

Something must always be given up. A head must be laid down on the block. A sacrifice made without any hope of return. At least, this was Fox-Owl's understanding when he first took on the mask. That there would be no turning back. That if he did indeed wish to get to that other shore, then once the mask was on that would be it.

It had taken some doing. There had been more than a few rounds of stepping up to the edge, testing the ground there, projecting—and planning—ahead. Standing at that rim and very occasionally looking over just in case he could see what was down there (although, of course, he suspected that things would always look different from the distance and from this side of things as it were).

The mask idea had come to him very late one night—in the witching hour, appropriately enough—when every other creature was fast asleep except him, soon-to-be-Fox-Owl, who was wide awake. He had had the sudden realisation—as if someone or something had whispered this message in his ear—that he would never be able to step over that edge (why would he choose his own demise?). This self that he had attended to carefully all his life was not capable of that final act. There might well be some shuffling around and about that edge—such toing and froing was a definition of sorts of his life to this point—but to really make that leap, to move forwards with no knowledge of what came next (and with no hope of return) would require something he did not have or require him to be something he was not.

But what if he were to become someone—or something—else? Take on a different role? The Fox-Owl came to him, softly and silently at that time. All of a sudden, there it was. An image in front of his eyes. Black triangular face. Large blue eyes. Blue feathers at the tips of its pointed ears. It offered itself up to him as if to say 'I'm yours, take me.' This image, it seemed clear, was something he might try on. Something of him, yes, but also not of him. Something that might just be able to take that final step.

Something must always be given up. It is only by this act that another way to proceed appears. Certainly, as Fox-Owl was only too aware, this required preparation. A setting oneself out to be opened up (hence the making of the mask). The making itself required a strange kind of will that undercuts the will. An embracing of one's own dissolution or, at least, a turn towards loss rather than gain. Perhaps even towards sadness rather than joy? But then what were all these but words? Labels for those feelings that came from an elsewhere—somewhere far far away—and that had always threatened (so it seemed to Fox-Owl) to sweep everything else away?

He already knew where he would need to go to find that edge once more. All it required was noticing specifically the places he had avoided. The places he did not want to go. To turn things around so that these darker landscapes would be somewhere that this particular Fox-Owl moved towards. This new figure would then live out that shadow side, follow its darker logics, attend to all that that he had previously and pointedly turned away from.

In this other darker landscape there was already certainly some of the stuff of his own previous self—his own business as it were—but, alongside this, or around and about it, was also something else. As if reconfiguring this work as a journey—and as a landscape of sorts—allowed for a laying out of all sorts of other figures and features. Other images and narratives and thus other options too.

And so, one day, it was this odd creature that stepped up to the threshold. An edge that was also, it was now clear, at the centre of his map. Be-masked and ready to go. And, with that, the leap over the mark was finally made.

And on the other side?

Well, a kind of non-place and non-space was how he later described it to anyone who happened to ask. In fact, more simply a change of point of view. Looking back over his shoulder he saw the act that he had previously been and, with that, all the other fictions that had sustained him but that, at times, had also dragged him down. And there with him at that time were also all the other Fox-Owls in a line. Each slightly different. Some with lighter blue feathers or a sharper face. Others with larger eyes or eyes with a reddish tint. All of them there looking on at this new arrival and nodding and tilting their masks or gesturing with head and hand.

Chapter 21: A King Under a Hill

Another beach and a body of water and then also other dark forms round and about. Are they trees perhaps? A forest even that comes nearly to the water's edge. A wind blows, but the black sea—or is it a lake?—is still and calm. There are other shapes nearby. Large black posts with something atop each of them. Something not to be looked at. And there are other dark but silver things on the shoreline that have been washed up. Are they dead fish? And then also other, larger things are there lying around and about. Or are they parts of things? In the sky there is a black sun encircled with fire or perhaps it's a hole where a sun should be. Whatever it is looks down on this barren scene with these four broken figures, each of them now arrived in that place that sooner or later everyone must visit.

No words are spoken but with a nearly imperceptible nod Fox-Owl gestures towards the shoreline and there they see a boat made of black wood pulled up on the beach as if ready to be boarded. They can see also some kind of figurehead at the prow, although it's difficult to make out the details or any features of the face in the dark wood. Fox-Owl begins the walk across the beach, feet crunching on small stones or shells (or could it be something else beneath his feet?). Ribbonhead follows, unsteady and stumbling somewhat, then Hare, nervously looking this way and that. John is the last to leave.

With scarcely a ripple the boat leaves the shore and glides across the black mirror-like surface. Fox-Owl stands at the prow, his mask staring straight out ahead. Besides him stands John, both hands tightly gripping the sides of the small vessel. Next is Hare, crouched in the middle, one hand nervously stroking the back of his neck. Finally, there is Ribbonhead, sat at the back, although there is no rudder there to be held and, it seems, no need to steer.

It is as a painting this scene, these tiny still figures, this small boat, all set against this wide black water and surrounding dark landscape.

And as they go it's clear that there are other things in the water that are around and about the boat and following in its wake. Occasionally they glimpse silvery scales and coils as whatever it is—or they are—breaks the surface.

Fox-Owl sees it first up ahead. A soft light of some kind, or, at least, a lighter grey drawn against the black. Dawn breaking perhaps? Or even a land mass? Fox-Owl points and all of them look towards the horizon line. In no time at all the line becomes a solid mass. It's an island, emerging out of what now appears to be a grey mist. An island with some kind of hill in its centre. As they get more close they can see that there is a small wooden jetty there at the island's edge reaching out towards them and then, on that, there is a post with a lantern that is giving out a soft golden glow. Even from the boat they can also see the grass, dark and still, but lighter than the ground of that other dark beach they have left behind.

The boat glides silently up to the jetty and halts. Then each of them, one by one, climbs out and on to this, the other shore.

*

The island is larger than it seemed from the water—from where they are now they cannot see the other side—and is, indeed, covered in grass. The hill in the centre is also larger than it first appeared and conical in shape with smooth sides and what looks like it might be a flat top. In front of them, leading from the jetty towards the foot of the hill is a chalk path set within a ditch that is perhaps waist high. And then up above they see a welcome sight. Stars shining in the sky and one or two familiar constellations although not in the familiar places. It also seems as if it is nearly morning as a faint line of pinkish-red can be seen as if brushed against the grey horizon that is visible beyond the hill. A full moon also looks down on them as they begin to walk this sunken track.

As they walk they hear bells, or, at least, some kind of ringing—faint, but audible—and, looking down at their feet see also that they walk now through a carpet of bluebells in full bloom. The colour, even in this soft dawn light, is bright and vivid, dream-like—and the smell so pungent it nearly overwhelms.

At the foot of the hill the path goes up, ascending in a steep spiral. It has been cut into the side of the hill and is broad enough for two to walk together though they walk in single file. As they climb they can see the landscape of the island below, mounds and ditches demarcating different patterns and designs—intricate and interlocking circuits and lines that connect it all up. Beyond this marked landscape there is the jetty with the orange glow and the water, though they cannot see that other black shore from here.

All at once the wind gets up again. It begins as a breeze, but is soon whistling around them, blowing their clothes close against their skin. It's cold but there is something that is clarifying in the thin air.

Eventually they reach the summit. It is indeed a flat plane with longer grass and a further smaller mound, ten foot tall or so, in the centre. The sun begins to show above the horizon line, lighting up the sky in a pink and orange glow and casting a deep shadow behind the mound. In the middle of that smaller mound it is suddenly apparent there is a large door.

A bell sounds again—this time louder—ringing out across that landscape and with that the door slowly opens inwards.

And now, as if hearing a further call, each of them steps forward and enters into the darkness. There are stairs that descend steeply. It's dark, but not too dark to see. Indeed, it seems as if there is a glow coming from whatsoever lies at the bottom of this passageway down.

There is a smell of cold earth and, alongside that, a sense of something very old.

As they make their way down, the glow below becomes brighter. It's bluish in colour. Cold, but not unwelcoming.

More steps down and they eventually arrive at the entrance to a large chamber hewn out of the rock. Smooth floor, ceiling and walls and with a stone throne set in the centre. On the throne there is a figure still as the stone around them with eyes closed and iron crown on head. In one large hand an orb is held tight against their lap and it is this object that is giving off the glow that lights each of their faces now. This figure is the same blue-grey colour, only slightly lighter than the grey of the rock that surrounds them all.

Then one by one, as if moved by an invisible hand, they take up their positions around the throne. All that is, except John who, looking around now, is nowhere to be seen. When did he go? And where? Was he there when they entered this chamber? Surely he was on the walk up the hill? Or, at least, on the jetty? Or was he? Did he even get off the boat? Thinking back, it's now less clear. Was there always only these three figures, Fox-Owl, Ribbonhead and Hare? But now, looking at this grey figure on its throne, there is something of John about them. Something about the furrowed brow, the heavy lids of the eyes and the shadows there. Could it be that there is a second John in this chamber?

This king on this throne is at a dark centre of sorts. Above the throne a mound of earth. A point in a landscape on a map of other points and places, other sites of travel between this world and others. And further above this, from the apex that is this throne, an inverted cone stretches out, within which there are other planes and other landscapes with various tracks and passageways between them all. And then above all this the stars. Other worlds, other universes even.

Around this king our three figures now stand. Hare seems taller somehow down here and more alert. Ribbonhead's colours are also more vivid and his head more straight. And as Fox-Owl reaches up and adjusts his mask which, here, seems larger and brighter, the same bell as before sounds. It's even louder this time and, it seems, is activating something old and slow. And now it is as if the world and the sky above are turning around this pivot point. This place is being connected to all those others out there—and to all those other figures, some of whom are rehearsing in a village hall, others of which are marking out a diagram on a rainy moor.

Ribbonhead shakes his head in a blur of colour and, once more, begins his jerky dance. He's circumambulating the throne as if once more being drawn along that other deep track. Hare lets out a laugh and then takes up his position and part following in Ribbonhead's wake. And Fox-Owl? His features are still hidden, but he is himself more regal somehow standing there. He reaches into his jacket pocket and out comes that script again. And then he's reading out aloud. It's something about four players on the road with various props and prompts. And then also some stranger parts about different devices and how they might be found or made. And as Fox-Owl reads and the other two dance, the bell rings out once more, and this other ancient device that sits before them opens one eye then the other. Awake at last.

Chapter 22: Repair

So, it's been raining for hours now. I say rain, but it's more or less sleet. I'm walking across another bloody boggy moor. My boots and socks are soaking wet. My jacket has soaked through and my clothes are freezing cold. I can't feel my fingers. Even my beard is bloody dripping. But guess what? I feel great. This is how I like it. Like how I feel when I enter a room and I know everyone in there dislikes me. It puts me at ease. I can breathe out and start to think. Work things out. So, on this moor, all is good. I can get a bit of clarity on things.

I've so much anger locked up inside me. It's like I'm on a short fuse all the time. I was once told that beneath anger is sadness. I don't know about that. Probably some truth in it, but it doesn't feel completely right, in my case anyway. Like when I'm on this moor. I feel alive. Fierce. It's like the anger is an energy, which I can then change perspective on. On the moor it's as if everything has been tipped ever so slightly and the anger turns into something else. This huge feeling of joy comes over me. And then I feel like things are beginning again. New horizons and all that. It's at these times that I feel like a king—King John!—and that all this—the moor, the rain, what's occurring inside and outside—all of that is mine. My kingdom. Like I've found that crown. Or as if it's been there all along, on top of my wet hair, but I've just not seen it. Or not wanted to see it for some reason.

Sometimes I laugh out loud when this happens. What a sight that must be. A big crazy brute laughing in the rain! That's maybe not a huge thing for you but, for me, there was a time when I had no memory of smiling, let alone laughing. So, something has shifted that's for sure.

And so I walk from moor to moor, careful to avoid other people. I've found that I'm a bit more centred when there's no one else around. When I do happen to pass close I can see folk eyeing me up suspiciously (and sometimes I'd say with a bit of fear) then moving away. I don't blame them. I'd be the same if I came across some big scruffy—and smelly—tramp, especially one who looked a bit crazy. I know how it goes. I find the things I need on the way. Some of it is stealing. I know, I know… but I figure my needs are more pressing than most and I never take more than I need or leave a farm or household without. On a night I'll bed down in some barn or outhouse, or, if out in the wilds, under a hedge or tree. It's odd, but despite the cold and wet, the further out I am—away from the towns and cities—the better I sleep. It's as if all that chatter crowds me out somehow. Don't get me wrong, there's scary stuff out here. And there are other kinds of chatter, if you get my drift. But despite the fear that sometimes comes down and surrounds me, it's also calmer and quieter.

One other thing. I've got something with me. It's in my backpack, wrapped up in some old ribbons I found round and about. A round silver orb. I don't recall how I came by it or why I keep it. I just have a sense it's for something. I realise that sounds odd. And that I'll know how to use it when the time comes. Sometimes, when things get really bad I'm tempted to throw it out, into a river or from the cliff tops into the sea. I feel like maybe it's the last thing that's holding me back (but holding my back from what? That's the question here). But keep it I do. No doubt it'll be buried with me, though, to be honest, I don't think there'll be anyone around to kick these old bones into any hole. Or to dig a hole for that matter.

Where am I heading? I'm not sure I'm heading anywhere. It's no hero's journey I'm on that's for sure. It doesn't feel like there's going to be any resolutions, at least for me at any rate. Sometimes, when I lie down after a long day's hike I can feel the end of it all in my body. It's like my bones are aching to get back into the earth. But for now the small fire is still in there, keeping me going.

I remember—way back when—that I used to perform. Sometimes there would be a costume and some paint for the face— and then that crown of course—but often it was just a change in view that would allow me to act something else out. I would

144

become these other characters, take on these parts that seemed to be in me but also come from outside if you can get your head around that. Or I could just get wild myself, stripped to the waist, howling at the moon and at whoever else was there. I think that's why I'd been given the job. At other times, I'd get on a line, repeat certain gestures, as if something else were animating me. It'd be hilarious. The audience could sometimes look, well, a little scared, but the rest of the crew would be in stitches. It was as if a wind had got up and caught my sails. I couldn't stop, each repetition more comic than the last. It would be like I was on the moor again (though, thinking about it, I only really started doing this walking after all that). There'd be something happening within me but also outside of me too. And me, I'd just be there, on the side-lines, watching as this other character took me on. Flailed me around a bit.

It's tricky to get some distance on all this and say how it is, it but let's just say that there are two of me—at least—in here. And that when one speaks—the one telling you all this now—the other watches or, sometimes, I fancy is just getting some kip.

And then there's this dumb wound I have that never seems to heal. A scab forms but always cracks and bleeds again. I can't remember how I got it. It feels like it's always been there. Like somehow I happened to it rather than it to me. It's this deep cut that keeps me alert. Focuses things. Reminds me that things will end, and then that the ending always comes too soon. It's also my connection to all this out there. It's like sometimes I think I am nothing but this cut that is somehow wrong, all messed up, but, with all that, also right. Or, as if my walking on this moor is somehow part of the repair that's needed and that what I'm doing with this journey is gathering things together to make something out of all this mess. Something to keep me on the right track or, perhaps, to switch me to another track.

*

I remember it like it was yesterday. We had gone to a place in town and as usual I had gone straight to the bar. And then—before I'd even ordered a drink—it started. Everything, quite suddenly, becoming unmoored…slipping away…then tipping. Or as if some strange fog—or a huge weight of sorts—had descended from nowhere. Something very dramatic and there, all of a sudden, in my experience. I remember clearly that was when the panic set in. I couldn't breathe. Or felt I couldn't. I needed to get out quickly. Find help. Or at least find the others. I got up from my stool and made my way, stumbling, to the door and then to the stairs leading to the floor above. Nothing seemed right. Everything was off kilter—as if I'd been punched hard—but no pain, nothing like that. There was just this incredibly intense feeling that I'd never felt before that something had descended but also dropped away from things. Or that I was drowning somehow and, again, couldn't get the air I needed.

And, with that, there was a massive anxiety. Overwhelming. As if this was it, the beginning of the end.

I remember hearing the music and seeing the shadowy figures in there. And then, quite suddenly, through no will of my own it seemed, I was dancing. As if I were part of some machine that had been activated. I was moving like I had never done before (at least it felt that way). It was pure joy. There's no other word to describe it. Then, looking up, two of the friends I had come with suddenly appeared, arm in arm, broad grins, themselves dancing in time with each other, moving together as if part of some fine mechanism or on some kind of swing. Everything was somehow off balance but also strangely in alignment. All correct. And then also this lack of fear—all that had subsided or been transformed—and, with that, a letting go. I remember laughing out loud.

I was hooked.

Later that same weekend we were out and about again, this time in an old quarry with a sound system all set up and ready to go. Once again, there was dancing, this time under the stars. I recognised faces from the night before (odd though that sounds). Suddenly the sound system that was there was cranked up louder and everything became activated. The stars and trees and others there with me. And all sorts of other people there too. Kids from the town. Travellers with tattoos. Someone with ribbons on their head. I know this will sound strange, unbelievable even, but there were animals there too—a hare and fox at least—standing up on their hind legs and dancing with us. And all of us there—I was absolutely convinced of this—were marking out some crucial diagram or pattern together.

This scene brought me back into contact with a landscape that was a place of my childhood. Very simply, I found myself there once more, amongst the trees and with the sweet smell of the ferns. Sun climbing higher into the sky after a long night. Everything immediate, just the seen in the seen. No chatter. No future projection.

There is a continuum between city and forest, from club to quarry and wood.

It was in one of these places that the name Fox-Owl had made itself present and been taken on. And not just him, but Frix-Cowl, Fux-Rowl and all the rest. All the other countless variations, the whole sequence. Different names crowding in one after the other. At that time I was so excited that I had scurried around introducing myself to everyone. All my brilliant new names, trying each of them on in turn. I remember some puzzled looks but mostly welcoming nods and smiles. This name—or series of them— seemed more appropriate to what was passing through me. So I took it—or them—on. Why not? Looking back, it was certainly a break from whatever it had been my lot to carry up to that point. Whatever it was that had been set up for me (and which, from this new perspective, well, just seemed like an old and worn-out story).

It was after all that, when the music, finally, had stopped, that I decided to leave the city and move to the country. I packed a few things and just walked out one bright morning. It took a while to get beyond the suburbs and other industrial estates and outlying buildings, but eventually I reached fields and then woodlands. On a night I'd bed down in a ditch by a hedge, or in a coppice. I would sleep well. Better than before. Even then, so soon after leaving, I knew I had done the right thing.

Eventually I made it to this place at the edge of this old oak wood. It's well away from any paths. I'd seen a hare the first morning here and knew, therefore, that this was a good spot. Here then, under the trees and in amongst the ferns, I built a bivouac and gathered a small circle of stones within which to make a fire. The nights are cold and, yes, sometimes frightening, but there is something about being outside in this landscape with the sky and stars above. Something about being connected to something I was part of but had become estranged from. There was a healing here, or, at least, some space that then seemed to allow things to settle and find their place. At times, sitting by my small fire, it was as if I could see the whole of my life—the different events and encounters, different concerns and desires—all laid out as on a tabletop. One shape, one pattern. Grasped all at once. And, with that, there was also an understanding that this map or picture of a landscape was superimposed on other maps of other places and then other times too. At those odd moments I would also get a sense of other figures, even those other Fox-Owls again, doing their thing—in their own woods and worlds—and that there was a connection of sorts to this long line, albeit this had been obscured by all the ins and outs, the many more trivial things that tend to foreground themselves (certainly in my life anyway).

It would be then that it would occur to me that this Fox-Owl character was a container of sorts. Or that my inner world was doubling the outer one and with the same wind blowing through both. And, as such, my inner journey was the same as the outer one I'd been on. It's difficult to explain, but it was something to do with how the narrowing down of my focus and my world to Fox-Owl's allowed this other broad expanse to come into view. As if, at the same time, I was both letting go of a particular self, but then also occupying a new fiction that was allowing other things to come in to focus. Indeed, beyond all that me, me, me something else was stirring. Something, as yet, unformed. Don't get me wrong, it wasn't as if I was discovering some hidden place or a secret self. Finding out who I *really* was or anything like that. More as if I had become involved in some kind of experiment, or even a construction project of sorts. Something at any rate that was yet to be fully written out.

*

I live in a small wooden house. Actually, it's more like a hut than a house. From my back door there is a path that runs to the sea. The path goes across a field, with a gate and a sign that says BEWARE OF THE BULL. There's no bull in the field, but it means no-one except me uses the path. I should say that it wasn't me who put the sign there, in case you're wondering. And when I say path, it's really just well-trodden grass.

Every morning, after a cup of strong tea, down I go to the rocks and to my special swimming spot, a place where I can lower myself into the water without too much bother. The surface of the water is always covered with seaweed, unless there's been a storm or some other very bad weather. It's always cold, bracing. I dip down, completely submerge myself, then come up and swim out beyond the rocks. Sometimes I turn and look back at the shoreline and at my home. I like this perspective, looking on as if someone else lives there. Seeing things from this other point of view. I fancy, sometimes, that this swim is the cure I need. That this seaweed which surrounds me is a better drug than the other ones I'm taking. Sometimes I duck back beneath the waves, hoping for some kind of transformation. It doesn't happen, but there is a kind of cleansing that happens. And the cold is certainly clarifying. It's like pressing a reset button.

Along the coast, perhaps three miles away, is the house where my friends live. There's three of them there. One always wears a kind of animal mask, though it's not of any animal I've encountered. He's called Fox-Owl and, at a pinch, you might say there's something of those two creatures in how he moves and in the features of the mask he always wears. Another always wears this hat of sorts with different coloured ribbons that hang down covering his face. He's a bit quieter than the others and is called Ribbonhead, which, I suppose, is accurate. Then there is a large man called John. He's a bit older and fierce looking, but he's very friendly. They all are, in their way. After my swim and another cup of tea I'll walk over there, sit with one or two or all of them. I listen to them talk about what they're up to. It's always interesting. The house is large and ramshackled, with some outhouses and sheds. It has a large kitchen with various mismatched chairs and assorted rugs. There's an old wood burner too that gives off a good heat. Everything looks as if it's seen better days, but I don't mind. It reminds me of my own place. We sit, drink more tea. John and Ribbonhead smoke roll-ups. As the day wears on the three of them start to talk about the performance they're planning—there's always stuff they've got coming up—and then there are rehearsals or, at least, we all move to another room that has various instruments and other equipment set up. Sometimes more recently I take up a microphone or play around with one of the pedals or other boxes on the table there. No one has ever suggested I do this or invited me in exactly, but it seems clear that it's OK.

And then sometimes I can lose myself in the sounds we all make together.

And when that special thing happens everything shifts, as if the whole house is tilting somehow. And, with that, other things come into focus. It's like all of us there, but also the various equipment—the different devices as I call them—are part of some larger machine that has started up and then clicked into gear. All the different components aligning together.

Everything in tune.

It's magical when this happens and time flies or, at least, hours go by without any of us noticing. For myself, when I'm standing in that place, sounds seem to come from nowhere, or, at least, from a somewhere else. Somewhere far far away. It might be that I have brought something with me. Some words on a scrap of paper, scribbled down when I have woken up from a dream in the middle of the night. But this is just a prompt to call up that other thing that then speaks through me if that makes any kind of sense.

Sometimes I wonder if this is perhaps enough. That what we have here, together, is as good as it gets.

The others have taken to calling me Hare. I don't mind. It's not my real name, but, then again, I never much recognised myself in the name I was given. Recently I've taken to wearing a costume of sorts or, at least, more colourful clothes and other small objects around my neck and waist. I also wear some paint on my face, not much, just some bright colour, a bit of blue or yellow perhaps and then sometimes a little glitter around the eyes and mouth. I'm not sure if this is preparation for something—perhaps I will perform with the rest of them?—but, anyway, it makes me feel, well, more myself. And more a part of what's happening if you know what I mean. Not that I especially feel like I have a self. That's always been part of the problem really, or even, perhaps, part of my illness. I experience myself more like a landscape to be honest. Or like the weather even. At any rate what I have described to you just now—the place I live and places I go—is a sort of a description of my internal state too. Or at least a region of it.

I know this will sound odd, but sometimes I think it's this other thing—that we are when we're together—that has summoned me here to be part of it. It's as if it has called on me from a future place to help make it (I know that sounds odd). Sometimes I think that, really, I have no say here. I'm just following some kind of script. I *think* it's me that makes decisions, for example, about what I'm going to do on a certain day but, every time, here I end up—after my swim—with these other three, in this particular arrangement or diagram as I've come to understand it. I never actually plan to make these visits but then visit I always do. I'm also never entirely sure what part I play. But I definitely seem to *fit* somehow. There's also something about how I partly recognise these three. If not from my dreams, then from someplace else, though I can never quite recall where that might have been. I can see the scars each of them has—we all have them of course—and I understand both the silences and their focus. There's not much talking, especially when the old device starts up, but I don't mind that at all. In fact, I prefer it. I think there's plenty of other communication going on. And then, of course, off we go on that line again, to a who knows where.

The sea and that house, here, in this landscape. Only a few places to go, but it's enough. In fact, I have learned—often the hard way—that less is more. That details—and, indeed, focus—matter. That all that is really needed for a life are a few images. Images that can orientate you. And that trust is important. You need to trust that others know their parts and that they can, if need be, carry you and yours. And that the process works and, indeed, is not just something for you alone. Indeed, that's the secret here. It's for all of us.

*

So, I arrived at this particular field one summer's day. I remember
the bees buzzing and the birds singing, and then also a gathering of
people there. Some stalls had been set up selling food, drink, other
bits and pieces, trinkets and the like. It was a warm day and the sun
was high in the sky. It was an idyllic scene, like a dream really.

And there was an air of expectation.

It was clear that something was being prepared for here.
Something was going to happen at this place on this day. Looking at
the faces as I walked around, I wasn't quite sure that everyone was
really prepared for whatever it was that was going to occur. Indeed,
more and more as I walked around, exchanging the odd greeting, I
felt that many were a little *un*prepared. I remember that at some
point the clouds moved to obscure the sun and a bit of a chill
passed over us all. At the same time, I sensed, below the frivolity—
could it be?—a hint of fear. Almost as if what was happening here
was a cover or set-up behind which something else, something
entirely different was assembling itself.

This sense—a kind of odd déjà vu—passed as I strode amongst
the stalls, but then returned, when all of a sudden in the middle of
all of this activity I saw a tall pole had been erected with ribbons
affixed in a knot at its very top. Seeing this, I felt a sense of unease,
that became increasingly pronounced as I surveyed the scene. I had
a growing intuition deep within me that something was on its way.
Something was going to occur here that was going to disrupt all
this. The more I looked around the more plain it was that no-one
else seemed to be feeling this sense of what, increasingly, could only
be called dread. Or, at least, they were hiding it well. But, yes, I was
sure now. It was going to be at this place, here, and very soon, that
something unwelcome was going to arrive.

Something awful that would spoil everything.

The sense of dread inside me increased. What was wrong with
everyone? Could they not see something awful was about to
happen? Someone—or something—was about to arrive to break all
this up and spoil everything! The anxiety was becoming
unbearable. It was making me sick and as I walked, then ran from

152

stall to stall I became unsteady, knocking into people and things, crying out, shaking people. I was losing it!

And it was then, with a sudden moment of absolute clarity—as if I was out of my body and looking down at this scene—that I understood.

It was me that had arrived.

It was me that was there to spoil everything.

Later, in that same field, they crowned me Ribbonhead. I don't remember much about the ceremony, but I vividly recall the feeling on my face as that soft brightly coloured fabric fell over it for the first time. I remember also my first few stumbling steps after I had assumed this role and then being lifted up high on two peoples shoulders I think it was. Or was it on a platform of sorts? And then being walked in some kind of procession along the ridge, with the sun now beginning to set behind me. Indeed, I could also *see* this scene, as if from afar or, at least, from up above. This train of figures, with me, carried, up front. And yet I still do not know where that vision came from, or how I was able to assume that perspective given that I was *in* the procession, my eyes hidden beneath blues, reds, greens and golds.

At any rate, I had been chosen, that much was clear. But for what? And who or what had chosen me?

Later still, I was told what had happened that day. I had passed out after wrecking the majority of the stalls and having knocked down at least half a dozen of those gathered there. I know I had been given something to drink as I can also still recall feeling lightheaded. Drunk even. I remember how good that felt! There was also some singing as I had been crowned—is that the right word?—with these ribbons and, thus, taken on my appointed function (whatever that might be). In fact, it didn't feel exactly that it was 'I' that was taking on this function and more that this function had taken on me. A baton had been passed on. Or there had been a renewal of sorts.

There was also a sense that something had been left behind in order to fulfil all this and that the awful scene at the festival (if that's what it had been, I can't be sure) had been part of this. Part of the hollowing out that would then allow this other thing to step forth and present itself. Certainly, when I did peer out from beneath the ribbons and caught a sight of myself in a window or, perhaps, it was a puddle or pond (strange, but I don't recall) I certainly didn't recognise what I saw. It was both me and not me. I was there, but also not there. In that mess of colour and taller somehow. Or at least less stooped that I had been before.

Then, after everything had been said and done, after everyone had laughed and got drunk and danced into the early hours—there was certainly a sense of relief in the crowd there after I had been crowned—and I had performed the various tasks assigned to me (many seemed comic, even absurd at times)… when finally everyone had gone to bed, I had, at last, some time on my own. In the light of a full pale moon I sat down with my back against an old Oak and with a drink in my hand I reflected on what I had become. A sign of some kind or a symbol of something? Certainly, a fiction of sorts, that much was clear. It suited me. Indeed, I think the match—between me, as I was, and this new guise—was a good one. It was then that I decided, or, perhaps I should say, Ribbonhead decided, to be, well, Ribbonhead. To take this mantle out and about. To see where it might lead. Possibly—I can't be sure—this had always been the plan (but then again, *whose* plan exactly?).

Chapter 23:
A Cut is Made, a Figure Appears

In a date in the future—but then is this also a memory from the past?—they are on a small stage in an old disused chapel on the mainland. The event has been locally advertised and there's quite a crowd. There's an air of expectation, even a slight nervousness that is there in the large hall. After a while the main lights go down and a couple of spots light up the stage. The performance begins quietly and without any announcements. Fox-Owl seems to be attending to various pieces of electronic equipment, some more recognisable than others. Certainly, there is a keyboard and then there are other boxes and pedals arranged around him. Hare is up there too. He's playing what looks like a recorder and then also occasionally stepping on some pedals to change the speed and tone of the sounds that are coming from the large speakers set up at either side of the stage. Ribbonhead is also there, standing quite still and looking more solid than usual. He's holding a microphone in one hand while in the other he holds some papers. He starts to read something out from this script, though his voice has been distorted somehow and is more gruff than usual. The others build up various loops and refrains around him.

After a while the sounds start to get more rhythmic and louder. And then, all of a sudden, it becomes very hectic indeed. There's a call and response that has started up between Hare and Ribbonhead. It's almost as if each is attempting to shout the other one down and yet, at the same time, the two voices coil around each other. It's not exactly a song they're singing, though some words can just about be heard. There's something about a journey through a landscape and a descent into a darker place. If you listen closely you can also hear Ribbonhead swearing under his breath, which is odd for him.

Ribbonhead then starts doing this strange dance. Arms and legs straight and at about a forty-five-degree angle to his body as he rocks back and forth on the balls of his feet and then also sways from side to side. Then, all of a sudden, he's jumped down into the crowd and then jumped up again onto some tables at the edge of the hall. He's leaping from table to table, shouting something about how there's going to be something going off tonight. About how something is going to arrive and then we'll see. It doesn't feel part of the performance at all. It's as if something else has come in and taken over. Everything suddenly feels unsafe or as if it's about to go out of control. There's even a hint violence in the air. A real sense of danger. And Ribbonhead is going crazier and crazier. Jumping around, banging the tables like some animal who's lost it.

And then he stops and is crouched down on one of the tables breathing hard. Everything is now in slow motion or as if something has somehow thickened the air. He reaches up with one hand and pulls the whole hat of ribbons off his head.

He's holding it up in his hand like some kind of limp dead animal or trophy perhaps.

And then the strangest thing.

The most shocking aspect of this whole scene.

It's John.

It's John's glaring face that looks out.

There's a lull in the sound and that figure that was Ribbonhead and is now John gets down off the table, crosses the hall and climbs back up on the stage. He grabs the microphone and shouts out loud as a bell.

'Where's the Dragon?'

The sound then starts up again, this time more urgent and at a faster pace, even more rhythmic than before. John shouts out once more, this time more loudly,

'Where's the Dragon?!'

The tune becomes more frantic, more chaotic as John shouts out his question again and again.

Where's the dragon?!

Where's the dragon?!
Where's the dragon?!
Where's the dragon?!
WHERE'S THE DRAGON?!
WHERE'S THE DRAGON?!

Then from the back of the dark hall, something appears. A mass of gold with a long pole poking up from one end. On the end of the pole is some kind of head that does indeed look like a dragon's, although it's also clear it's simply a painted wooden cut out. The body starts moving in time to the music, then in and out of the crowd gathered there, the pole pumping up and down, up and down.

It's quite a sight. Like some kind of crazy amateur dramatics.

The dragon progresses towards the stage, weaving in and out of the crowd, its head bobbing up and down and swaying from side to side in time to the sounds coming from the front. The gold of the body is simply a piece of gold material wrapped around one, perhaps two figures. It's like some giant pantomime horse. It's all on an edge. All just about to collapse. But then it doesn't. And because it's not collapsing, it sails that edge, tacks into that wind. Moves more quickly because it sails so close.

John is also swaying from side to side again now, more gently than before, but almost mechanically, arms straight and moving up and down, by his side. Hare is standing still, microphone in hand, calling out various names it seems. And all the while Fox-Owl is focused on the various instruments and other devices up on that stage, pushing them further and further, allowing them to work back on all this, to tell him—and the others gathered there—where they need to go.

And from out here, it looks as if the whole set-up has in fact been planned somehow. As if this thing that is now suddenly here had called back to all of them from some future time so that they might gather and enact it. And, as always, this is the puzzle of it all. From this side of things, there is the struggle and the practice. The fumbling around in the dark. And then, when finally it's done, it's as if it had already been done or was always going to be like this. In fact, could be no other way. All the incidents and encounters. The images and other figures along the way. The frustrations and, yes, the drinking too. All of it, seemingly with a purpose that was already foretold. And these four—if we can presume that it is indeed Ribbonhead wrapped up in that gold cloth—are now following another assignment that has simply used them as its own device.

And there it is, apparent to those who are on the look out for such things. A second dragon that doubles the wooden one still dancing there. A dragon that sits beneath all this and always has done. And it is this other dragon that stretches its huge wings, turns, takes off and begins its climb into the sky.

Chapter 24: The Way Out is Further in

In that same quarry where we previously met this figure, here is Ribbonhead once more. Has he just come back from somewhere else or did he in fact never leave? At any rate, this time he is certainly more active. In fact, he's working hard. His ribbons seem brighter now and catch the sunlight as he works to erect a scaffolding of sorts. Poles are lifted onto shoulder then pushed and screwed into holdings. Planks are slotted across. If you listen closely you can hear him out of breath (it's heavy work and he's not exactly in shape). Bit by bit something is taking shape here although it's not entirely clear what it is or what it might be for.

The top of the structure is beginning to jut up and out above the quarry cliff now as Ribbonhead carries the heavy planks up the steps to make a platform at the very top.

Finally, when all's done, Ribbonhead walks out along the planks to the very edge of this structure he's built.

There he stops and stands absolutely still. His arms are straight down by his sides, head ever so slightly tilted. Could it be that he is listening out for some signal perhaps? Some transmission sent from some other place (it wouldn't be the first time, as we know)?

It's getting darker now and, behind and above him, constellations of stars are becoming visible in the dusk. There is a whole cosmos moving at its own scale and pace around this figure in this quarry on this platform, a centre point around which it all turns.

*

Ribbonhead is making an attempt to reach out beyond the context he is in and outside the script he has been given. All things considered, it's not surprising that he's making such an attempt. A set-up of some kind is certainly needed for this kind of work. This figure standing on this platform, darker ribbons now obscuring his face, announces, if nothing else, that there is always a foreground and background. And, as such, that there is always another fiction that might be taken on.

*

Just where the pine trees come down to meet the sea. On top of some sand dunes but in a shallow dip away from the wind. There is Hare busying himself with preparations for a small fire. He has already combed the nearby beach and forest floor for fuel. Sun bleached twigs and branches, the occasional piece of dried out driftwood or plank. He's piling it all up next to a small circle of stones he's put in place. When all has been gathered and after a brief rest to catch his breath, he carefully assembles a cone of twigs, then lays on the other bits of wood, each bigger than the last. Then, with some dry gorse and a match, he sets the small pile alight. Hare sits back and away from the smoke. He looks at the flames as they flicker and curl around the wood and at the sea and the sunset behind. He smells the gorse bushes and pine trees that are close but not too close to risk being set alight. Smells too the burning driftwood and the dusk. He hears the crack of the dry wood burning and also a breeze that rustles the treetops there.

And then, after a while, there is less and less thought. It is as if everything around him begins to settle down in this place. His surroundings take on a brightness. A thereness.

It's all a scene that has been laid out just for him.

And it is here and at this moment that Hare understands—if that's the right word—that there is nowhere to go and, in fact, no one in particular to be. He has passed through something—some gate perhaps?—and, looking back, sees himself, this figure Hare, crouched by this fire. Such a small but precious thing. It occurs to him then and there that this Hare has indeed been a fiction, one that has kept him on a certain path. And that this gate—now open—had been there with him all along.

Something so obvious. Hidden in plain view.

And now when Hare looks out at this fire and the shore lit up by the setting sun it's as if he looks out from nowhere. Or he fancies, it is as if there is a hole within the world which is also him (the hole is where his head should be). And with all this he lets out a chuckle. At last he can see the comedy of it all. His needs and wants and hopes and fears. The places he has moved towards and away from. All of those habits that have made him what he is and determined the contours of the world he has moved through.

*

There is a project here thinks Hare and not-Hare. To stake out the landscape of a given self. To look back at this self after going through the gate. To see it all laid out like a map or landscape with its different features and figures. And to look carefully at each of these. To see what position and place they hold and what narratives might connect them all. To see where they might lead and what they might say once they have also been given a little space to breathe.

*

All the green was reaching out to John. The trees and ferns. The fields in the distance and a further wooded ridge. All of it was suddenly right there. Looking at this scene in front of him he noticed a horse way off in a meadow. But then it was as if the horse were also right by him. He could hear the galloping hooves and the whinnying as if it had been transported to him or him to it (although he knew it was at least a mile or so away). And then he noticed something else. A face—or the suggestion of one—in the branches of an old oak. Glittering and twinkling, large golden eyes and a broad smile. Some kind of entity that seemed to be saying something along the lines of:

'Yes! This is it John!'

All this closeness and greenness and this grinning face. And, with that, an intense feeling of pleasure welling up inside. Just to be here, now, in this landscape. He laughed out loud. In fact, couldn't stop laughing. All of it was so funny, or not funny exactly, but

161

somehow preposterous and out of kilter. But also, strangely correct. Looking up at the blue sky, clouds like cut outs superimposed one on another. John had the sudden sense that he could at any time ask whatever this entity was to show him the way.

Later, walking along the old trackway, he meets a double of himself. A battered old van, doors open, stove and chair outside. And sitting there was this other John, bottle of beer in hand. This figure calls out 'It's not a bad day, eh?' and then 'Enjoy it!' Later still and walking past the other trucks on the track, the smell of woodsmoke and sound of music, and a lanky, hunched figure, lurching from door to door. He had the sense that he had also found Ribbonhead here, hidden amongst the vehicles.

*

It occurred to John then that the entity he had seen or somehow felt was not a being exactly but the green fire personified. And that it had seen him, welcomed him and then, as it were, laid out this further fiction for him as if to say, there you go—as you dreamt it, so it is. The world was unfolding these characters for him. Reflecting back his desires in concrete form.

*

Fox-Owl sometimes thought of his body as a landscape. A single landscape, but then, at other times, a collection of different landscapes too. Relating to himself in this way allowed him to do some detailed work. When he was able to focus right down then all sorts of insights occurred and some repair work became possible. Certainly, being both this landscape and its visitor allowed a flexibility in approach.

On one of his journeys down there into those hills and valleys he fancied he had seen a figure like himself alongside three others he thought he recognised. From a dream perhaps? There they were, on a dark moor. At that time—lost as he was—he had had an urge to reach out. To speak to them. To understand what they were enacting down there (certainly it felt significant).

162

At other times he would feel trapped by this body-landscape circuit, especially when he lost this ability to shuttle between points of view. At those times the external vista corresponded so exactly to his internal ones that he would become confused or, at least, unsure about which was internal and which external. As if, in fact, they were the same with just a slight trick, a slight raising up then folding back, giving the impression, or illusion, of a self.

After leaving the city he had moved into this old caravan at the edge of a wood. There he had at last hung up his mask—and put the other props away—and, with that, got down to the serious business of exploring his own landscape which was, after all, the place in which he lived. Who knows? Perhaps on his next trip *down there* he would see some important detail he had previously overlooked.

*

And down there it looks as though there are events unfolding, narratives even, within these other places. A trip to another shore. A figure in the centre of it all under a hill. As if all of this—laid out—is on a map that has now come into focus. A place, not exactly of memory—many of these things never happened, could not have happened or, indeed, are set somewhere way beyond where Fox-Owl is lying back on an old, battered couch. But these images have arrived from somewhere. They have been asked to be written out and presented here.

Coda

The truth is there are times when I wonder how things might have been. If I'd done this or that or taken this or that road. Maybe had put on that crown so to speak. But mostly I'm content. I like coming here every day. Not having to go other places. Not having to answer to other folk. I treat it like a job. I get here early, before six. I stumble around in the dark with my cup of tea, leave the house and make my way down here to my hut. To get started before the sun is up, that's the trick. To get a bit of a jump on the day.

My place is a bit of a mess to be honest. I've accumulated a lot of things. Books, ornaments, trinkets. Quite a few empty bottles and cans I'm ashamed to say. An old pole I found on one of my walks that's leaning up against the desk next to a toy wooden sword. A silver sphere I picked up somewhere I can't quite remember. I've got that on a shelf above the desk. I've always liked the way it reflects my room back to me as if it's someplace else. There's stuff hanging on the wall too. Pictures and postcards, necklaces, a tattered golden cloak and blond wig. A painted wooden crown there on a nail. There's also this hat that's hanging next to it that's made of ribbons—however strange that sounds—from some other time and place. Stuff that's been given to me or that I've found (or that's found me). I'm sticky in that way. The books are research. Well, everything in the room is really. It's not like I've read many of them. It's really just about having them all gathered there. I'll look along the shelves, take one or two down, prop them on my desk. It's often just the covers that give me the inspiration. Summon a world as it were. In fact, I think it would be true to say that my room is itself a kind of world that nests these other worlds within it. Either that or it's a box of props for some performance or other (whatever that turns out to be).

Sometimes I like to make things when I'm down here and have finished everything else off. Often it's something out of words. Some kind of text, script, or what have you. Inventing characters, along with the journeys they might be on or speeches they might make. At other times I might draw something. A sketch of a face or a figure. Sometimes a landscape. At other times I'll have go at a diagram or perhaps a map. It's not very often—nowadays—that I'll do anything else. Very occasionally I'll get some of the old gear out—I keep it in an old, battered suitcase on the top shelf—and plug it all in then fiddle around with some peddles and loops. Just for old time's sake really. But it can still transport me all the same. Take me back to that other place. It's partly just the sounds the various instruments make that sets off the memories. I can be sat here, on my own in my hut and then—all of a sudden—I'm in a field or a quarry. Or a village hall. Or even back by that other place by the sea. There are other figures there with me. There's noise. Laughter. Memories of dancing in a field. Feelings suddenly arrive that are associated to that particular space and time.

Sometimes the dragon even makes a call.

Funny to think he's still there somewhere, round and about.

The drawings I do help me with the writing. It's as if they somehow pin things down more tightly. It was like this when I kept a diary. I could write pages and pages which, when I looked back at them, didn't really mean that much. But then, occasionally, I'd do one of these little sketches—maybe of something I'd seen, or something I'd dreamt. However rough it was it would somehow have caught that moment more completely than any writing, not least as it could be grasped all at once. It's as if anything done in that space and time, especially if it's drawn, has something of that space and time entangled in it or with it, if you get my drift. Anyhow, these drawings and my notes I keep in careful piles on the floor, with either a stone with a hole or maybe a bit of old driftwood to weigh them down. It's all research.

I don't mind talking about the old days, but, actually, it doesn't hold a lot of interest for me. It's not that I'm keen to forget, more that there always seems to be more going on where I am right now. Other stuff to focus on. If I do think about the past it's more as a kind of resource for something I'll be getting on with in the present. As if the past is just a particular set of images that are available. Or as if the past is a kind of landscape containing other things—other pathways and passages—that might still be open. I think that's why I keep this stuff that surrounds me. All these different objects, texts, and drawings pinned up on the wall. They all hold memories—some of which aren't even mine. They're like details that have moved from one world to another and, as such, for me, they allow for some travel. Even some transformation. This is what magic is for me. The ability to move. To shuttle from one perspective to another. And it's like in order to be able to do this— to occupy, as it were, those other fictions—I need some props and bits of scripts to work with.

I'm sure there's other ways and means. Perhaps stripping things back. Carrying as light a load as possible. But, for me, it's about the details. It's the details that make the fiction *work*. Allow it to be activated. It's not exactly a project of self-analysis as most of it is made up. But it is a question of seeing what's in there. What is making itself known. What needs to be heard or followed? It's as if I'm mapping something out but will only know what once I'm done. And then—as you'll no doubt appreciate—there's also the other small detail that I'm an invention too. Another figure that is also in another landscape, maybe even in its centre (at that dark spot as it were). Certainly this fiction that I am is rubbing shoulders with those other characters. Maybe even walking some of the same roads? That's the rub. I'm both in it and not in it at the same time. Or, as I often think when I wake up early and sometimes last thing at night: I'm making this ancient device, but it's also making me.

About the Author

Simon O'Sullivan teaches at Goldsmiths College, University of London, where he is Professor of Art Theory and Practice. His writings are mostly located at the intersection of contemporary art practice, performance and philosophy. He has published widely in these areas, often in relation to Gilles Deleuze and Félix Guattari and, more recently in relation to fictioning and myth-work.

His most recent monographs are *From Magic and Myth-Work to Care and Repair* (2024); *On Theory-Fiction and Other Genres* (2024) and (written with David Burrows) *Fictioning: The Myth-Functions of Contemporary Art and Philosophy* (2019). *The Ancient Device* is his first novel.

His collaborative art practice – with David Burrows, Alex Marzeta and Vanessa Page, and sometimes with others – comes under the name Plastique Fantastique, a 'performance fiction' that involves an investigation into aesthetics, subjectivity, the sacred, popular culture and politics produced through, performance, film and sound work, comics, text, installations and assemblages. Plastique Fantastique have performed and exhibited widely in the UK and abroad and are represented by IMT Gallery in London.

Other writings can be found at:
www.simonosullivan.net

And an archive of Plastique Fantastique work at:
www.plastiquefantastique.org

About Triarchy Press

Triarchy Press is an independent publisher of books about, amongst other things, radical, hypersensitised and misguided walking, walk-performances, performance and somatics. They include:

A Sardine Street Box of Tricks ~ Crab Man & Signpost
Anywhere ~ Cecile Oak
Before the Curtain Opens ~ Kate Kelly
Body and Performance ~ Sandra Reeve
Counter-Tourism: The Handbook ~ Phil Smith
Covert ~ Phil Smith & Melanie Kloetzel
Desire Paths ~ Roy Bayfield
Mythogeography ~ Phil Smith
Nature Connection ~ Margaret Kerr & Jana Lemke
On Walking and Stalking Sebald ~ Phil Smith
Rethinking Mythogeography ~ John Schott & Phil Smith
Stone Talks ~ Alyson Hallett
Terminalian Drift ~ Jerry Gordon
The Architect-Walker ~ Wrights & Sites
The Footbook of Zombie Walking ~ Phil Smith
The Long Way Home ~ Timothy Herwig
The MK Myth ~ Phil Smith & K
The Pattern ~ Crab & Bee
The Pilgrimage of Piltdown Man ~ Mike O'Leary
The Roots of Amerta Movement ~ Lise Lavelle
walk write (repeat) ~ Sonia Overall
Walking Art Practice ~ Ernesto Pujol
Walking Bodies ~ Helen Billinghurst, Claire Hind & Phil Smith
Walking for Creative Recovery ~ Christina Reading & Jess Moriarty
Walking Stumbling Limping Falling ~ Alyson Hallett & Phil Smith
Walking's New Movement ~ Phil Smith
Ways to Wander ~ Claire Hind & Clare Qualmann